Books by Ki Longfellow

China Blues
Chasing Women
Stinkfoot, a Comic Opera (with Vivian Stanshall)
The Secret Magdalene
Flow Down Like Silver: Hypatia of Alexandria
Houdini Heart
Shadow Roll: A Sam Russo Mystery Case 1
Good Dog, Bad Dog: A Sam Russo Mystery Case 2
The Girl in the Next Room: A Sam Russo Mystery Case 3

Follow Ki Longfellow on the Internet:

Blog kilongfellow.wordpress.com
Facebook Ki Longfellow
Twitter @KiLongfellow
Official Website www.kilongfellow.com
Sam Russo www.eiobooks.com/samrusso

Shadow Roll

by
Ki Longfellow

A Sam Russo Mystery

Case 1

Eio Books

This is a work of fiction. Though based on the known facts of people and places
mentioned, the events and characters inscribed herein spring from the author's
imagination. No descriptions of public figures, their lives, or of historical personages,
are intended to be accurate, but are only included for the purposes of writing a work
of fiction, and are not necessarily true in fact.

Copyright © Ki Longfellow 2013
All rights reserved.

Published in the United States by

Eio Books
P.O. Box 1392
Port Orchard, Washington, 98366 U.S.A.

www.eiobooks.com

Library of Congress Cataloging-in-Publication Data

Longfellow, Ki,
 Shadow roll : a Sam Russo mystery CASE 1 / Ki Longfellow.
   p. cm.
 ISBN 978-1-937819-00-2
 1. Private investigators--Fiction. 2. Staten Island (New York, N.Y.)--Fiction. I. Title.
 PS3562.O499S47 2012
 813'.6--dc23

                    2012007580

Cover designed by Shane Roberts
Book designed by Shane Roberts
Cover photo by Shane Roberts

Dedicated to
Humphrey Bogart & Funny Cide

(And to my beloved grandfather, Lindsay Ray Longfellow, who
took a seven-year-old off to the races.)

Shadow Roll

A Sam Russo Mystery

Case 1

"You don't wanna look," he said.

I said, "I've seen it all before."

He said, "Not this you ain't."

I looked anyway. He was right. Three years, more or less, after a war waged over what seemed the whole world, and I'd seen a few things, things I hoped never to see again, but I'd never seen anything like this.

The headache I'd woken up with got worse.

It was already one of those days. Some sick sonofabitch had decided to deliver a baby the easy way.

Delivery room was in one of those stands of red sumac, the kind that grows all over New York. As tenacious as pigeons, or drunks, this clump had struggled through cracks in the courtyard of a building Dickens could only dream of. The beat cop, guarding the courtyard entry, decided he needed to tell me the massive red brick heap began as a charitable infirmary, and ended as an orphanage.

"But now the kids are shunted to the top two floors to make way for the poor saps back from the war. You know, the one's so bad off they ain't never gonna see the outside again."

The beat cop looked about as old and as smart as a kewpie doll, yet he was already losing his hair. Wispy dishwater brown, with a comb over. On his wet upper lip a moustache struggled to grow. The thing was shaped like a tongue depressor. He was also wasting his rummy's breath. I knew more about the charity this place dished out than he ever would. For one thing, I was born here. And for another, I was raised here. The fact I survived here said a lot about me. The fact I'm not what you'd call a really nice guy said a lot about the Staten Island Home for Children. On the other hand, maybe that was just me. Sam Russo, born anytime, raised anywhere, pain in the ass. But even a pain in the ass, like every other joe back from Luzon fighting the Japs on horseback, was a hero. And that's a fact. Who knows how many of us scrambling to stay alive were ever seen again.

I got lucky. I missed the Bataan Death March because my horse had more wits than I did. Of course, by then, I had enough wits left to fill a shot-glass.

Which means I survived. I could of bought a little house on the G.I. Bill, filled it with a cute little wife and maybe a couple of cute little kids. I could of built a rabbit hutch out back—but I didn't want a rabbit. Before and after the war, I wanted to be a jockey. Trouble was, even when I was still a kid, I was always too big to be a jockey. So then I wanted to be a private dick. That idea came from sitting in the dark at the Paramount over on Bay Street watching *The Maltese Falcon*. Bogie's Sam Spade made it look classy, not to mention maybe lucrative. Besides, it was either that or cadging an acting job at Fred Scott's Movie Ranch miles away at South Beach. Fred's would of been second on my list if gumshoeing didn't pan out—except the movies moved west about thirty years ago.

These days, you had to be Seabiscuit to get a decent job.

Meanwhile, what me and everyone else were looking at was as rare as a Fair Deal out of Truman. Murder on Staten Island. A real live dead double homicide. Both the mother—couldn't be more than fourteen, if that—and the baby, no age at all, were spread out like garbage on a heap of collapsed sumac. They were in a courtyard stinking of piss, the sour reek of beer our homegrown Germans were busy brewing all over the city of Stapleton, and the sweet scent of tender flesh slowly sliding towards decay. They'd been there for a week, maybe more. The never-to-be-mother had that look Halloween pumpkins get just before they collapse in on themselves.

No pretending it was suicide. Suicides jump, but I'd never heard of one first open themselves up with a saw. Or sock their own jaw hard enough to knock out a tooth or three.

When I couldn't look anymore, about two seconds tops,

I turned away, cupped my hands to keep the wind in from the sea from blowing out my match, and stared through smoke at the Manhattan skyline. Five miles away, it looked pretty good. Haloed in light, it looked like life. But then, considering—pure pathos at my feet, "home" one whole shabby room with shared bath over a Rexall on the corner of Victory Boulevard and Bay Street, a headache getting worse by the minute—anything would.

When I turned back, a local photographer, moonlighting with the cops, was taking snaps with a fancy instant camera. A coupla more cops were wandering around in the small maple woods that grew on three sides of the building. And my old friend Lino, the guy who'd ruined my usual troubled sleep, was nosing about in the rubble and rust of the courtyard. Me, I was slowly following the bricks up the curved side of one of four towers; there was one of these on each corner of the Staten Island Lock-up for Innocent Kids. I did this until I was looking straight up.

I said, "Lino?"

"Yeah, Sam?"

"I think you'll find this didn't happen here."

"Yeah, Sam? So where did it happen?"

I pointed. "Up there somewhere." And then I looked down at what I didn't want to see. Seeing felt like a tearing away of the tendons that held my heart in place. "And then they were thrown away. Out a window maybe. A high window. But probably off the roof."

Lino did exactly what I'd just done. Looked up. Looked down. "Damn."

Then I said—because it was either that or bawl in front of a bunch of grown men—"And down will come baby, mother and all."

2

I was born to be a shamus. First off, I was already a dedicated snoop and second, I'd named myself Sam. And though Russo wasn't as much of a calling card as Spade—as in "digging up dirt"—it was the best I could think of after the Sam part. Third, I went to the movies a lot. I'd go see anything with cops and robbers. Before Bogie, I could of wound up a crook thanks to Jimmy Cagney. Seven, eight years old, I loved Cagney as much as I loved horses, specifically race horses.

First time I saw him was in *The Doorway to Hell*. He wasn't the lead actor, can't even remember who was—all I saw was Cagney. Then there was the *The Public Enemy*. Other stuff too, but *Angels with Dirty Faces* and *The Roaring Twenties* did it for me. He had this way about him, cocky and jumpy and tough as nails. But then I saw *The Maltese Falcon* and never looked back.

It wasn't that I stopped loving Cagney, I still loved Cagney; it was because I knew I wasn't cut out to be a crook. I didn't like stealing things or pushing dames around or hurting people. What I liked was poking my nose into things, asking questions, working out puzzles, making a nuisance of myself.

So when I got my PI's license and bought my 1947 model snub nosed Colt .38, a gun I was good with—thanks to using guns so much in my part of the world's slaphappy little war—I thought it was going to be all sleek-looking women, a lot of smart and sassy backtalk, and a mysterious black bird worth enough to chase from one exotic country to the next. Turned out, it was following some guy's wife to a seedy hotel in Factoryville, or blending in with the staff in one of Stapleton's breweries so we'd all find out who was taking home too much hootch. Staten Island, from top to bottom and side to side, was about as crime ridden as the jolly old Land of Oz. When the double homicide turned up, I'd already been planning a move to Manhattan or Brooklyn, maybe even a hop across the Kill Van Kull to Bayonne.

Damn. Where'd that last idea come from? It couldn't of come from me; had to be a fleeting fancy. Bayonne? Not on your nellie. More like Long Island halfway between Aqueduct and Belmont. Find a place on Rockaway somewhere, then just shuttle back and forth between the two race tracks.

But not yet. A killing on the island was attracting every cop for miles around. It was like a copper's holiday.

You could ask why a lowly PI was one of the first on the scene and I'd give you a true answer. Because I wasn't the only one born and raised in the heap of filthy red bricks and turrets Bela Lugosi would of scaled sideways. Once upon a time, Lino was locked up in there with me. But there's a truer answer. Lino Morelli was two years older, he had maybe three inches on me in height and thirty pounds in weight, but his brain was the size of a boiled carrot. Even so, he was Italian. As soon as I met him I'd decided I was Italian, although neither of us knew if we even had humans for parents. And now that big dumb Italian kid was a detective with the Staten Island Police, which was quite a few rungs down from the lowliest New York City precinct (maybe a whole ladder full of rungs), but police nonetheless.

On the north end of the island—the business end, so to speak—Lino Morelli was law.

So with us being practically brothers and me being the smart kid between us, here I was.

This was how smart Sam Russo was. I was here but there was no twenty-five bucks a day plus expenses at the end of it. There was no client, no money, and no credit. This was all on Lino's tab, and so far, all I'd ever gotten "working" with Lino was getting to read all about it in the Staten Island *Advance*. Lino Morelli, all round great cop and homegrown hero, comes up aces. Again. And now this sad mess. Lino and I never said a word between us, but we both knew I was supposed to solve it. Like usual. What the hell. I'd give it my best shot, but in my heart I was already gone. First choice: Manhattan, where, polite as a doorman and happy as a banker's son, I'd be high stepping over sidewalk drunks.

A few minutes later me and Lino and about a dozen other SI cops were peering at the woman who'd opened the front door after Lino pounded on it. Not only was the door engraved on my mind, so was the woman. She was a lot older now, but then, who wasn't? Age hadn't taken her down a notch. She was still tall, wide and grim.

We all got the evil eye. And the usual graceful greeting.

"What's goin' on? Get outta here! Don' choo know where you are? We got sick men in here."

Lino said, "Now ain't that the truth? You wanna let us in, Flo, or you wanna — "

That was as far as he got. Mrs. Florence Zawadzki knew the ropes from a long life of social services and cops. She moved aside with enough ill grace to allow us all to pass in. In my case, it was more like passing out. Stepping through that door was like falling down a well. The smell alone— boiled cabbage, soiled bedding, and furniture polish—was all it took to bring me "home" again. I stifled the words trying to come out of my mouth. Something was trying to say: "Hello, Ma." Fucking ironic. Old Flo knew as much about mothering as a cow knew about driving a cab.

I nodded at Mrs. Florence Zawadzki. The only thing I got back was the usual dirty look. Seems I was as welcome as ever.

Once inside, Lino never shut up. Which got Mrs. Z so flustered and defensive, her hearing she had two dead bodies in her shrubbery, I had a chance to slip away and do a bit of sleuthing on my own.

3

I knew every scuff mark, every initial carved in every table (I mean hell, a couple were mine), where every creak was in every floor board, every detail of every framed picture of Jesus—and every single one of 'em the spitting image of Alan Ladd in a toga. No getting away from Jesus in Flo's world. If he wasn't watching us eat, he was watching us sleep. I could name the rats. OK, so they weren't the same rats; I could name their distant ancestors.

Only the architect himself knew what he thought he was doing when he designed this heap. This was Staten Island, not the back lot at Universal.

There's a few things Staten Island always had enough of. Woods and hills were two of them. Especially on the outskirts of Stapleton. Sometime back before the invention of bread, a load of rich do-gooders had taken over a few acres of both—someplace that'd once been someone's farm and before that stolen from the natives by the Vanderbilts—and there, they built the Staten Island School for Children.

Growing up, I remember wondering why charity buildings all looked like prisons. Or fortified castles. Or haunted hotels. Or English madhouses. It didn't take me long to figure it out. Because they were. Even if your crime was being born into poverty and then getting dropped at the door in a cardboard box. That was Lino's mistake. Or having a kid for a mother. And her raped? Willing? Her own father? Her brother? An older tough on the block?

Who knew. Girl gets shoved in for a week, dumps the baby, gets taken away again.

That was my mistake.

In any case, I never knew who she was, where she came from or where she went. Over the years, I'd thought about her a lot. Wondered if she ever thought of me. If she ever regretted leaving me behind. Probably not. Out of sight, out of mind. By now she no doubt had three more brats and was living in a cold-water walk-up in Queens. But I liked to think she made it somewhere. Maybe even the movies. I liked to think that a lot.

Not knowing who she was, I never knew who I was. So, just like I made her up, I made me up, including the name. Sam Russo, gumshoe. And here, finally, was my first chance at a killing.

I was up all five flights of stairs before anyone noticed.

The rummy of a beat cop was right. Every orphan in the place was crammed up here like bodies stacked in a morgue. Beds in a row, no more than a foot between each. Personal belongings in cardboard boxes under the bed. A picture of Alan Ladd aka Jesus on the otherwise bare wall over each bed. More smell of cabbage and piss, only stronger.

My headache got worse.

I was being stared at by every kid in the joint. Staring back, I was looking for the big mouth, the kid who'd push himself forward to impress all the others, the one who'd start telling me tales. In other words, I was looking for the kind of kid I was. There's always one. Turned out this one was a girl.

"Whatchoo doin' here? You ain't a cleaner or nothin'."

I pointed at the door I'd just come in. "Across the hall, two doors along, that was my room. Mine and Lino's."

"Git outta here, Mister. This building ain't as old as you."

"You kiddin'? This place was here when Columbus showed up."

While I was saying that, I was also moving fast towards the big multi-paned windows that looked out over where a kid like these kids had come sailing by a while back, a fully formed babe still in her belly. Mrs. Z was down there making a hell of a racket. In one second flat, not only me, but every other kid in the room was pressed up against the grime of old glass trying to see why.

"Any of these windows open?" I asked loudmouth.

"I thought you said you lived here?"

"Times can change."

"Where'd you hear that? I been here since I can't even bemember and all the windows always been shut. With nails. Big ones."

So the Zawadzkis finally got wise. Took 'em long enough to figure kids were using the windows, even the highest windows, to escape.

Far below, Lino was showing Mrs. Z the bodies. In response, Mrs. Florence Zawadzki was screaming. And would you look at that—Mr. Zawadzki was down there too. From up here, I couldn't tell how he was reacting, but Flo's lesser half: caretaker, gardener if he ever bothered which he seldom did, bed warmer, and general handyman, was standing off by himself, looking on. Flo was clutching Lino, not Mr. Zawadzki.

Back in my day Mr. Zawadzki was small but wiry; he looked smaller now. None of us had ever known his first name. We called him what Flo called him: Mister. Which reminded me.

"What's your name, kid?"

"Bonnie Jean. I'm only eight so don't go thinkin' nothin' funny."

That knocked me back on my heels. First, because there wasn't one thing funny about any of this. Second, what put that in her head? To the kid I was, "funny" meant sneaking a smoke in the store rooms behind the kitchen. Funny could even mean hiding in the Zawadzki's closet hoping to see something. I don't know about anybody else, but I never did.

I looked at her straight. "So far, I haven't seen anything to laugh at around here."

A kid behind her, red hair stuck up like a whisk broom, said, "You got that right. Who's down there? Is that Pamela?"

I'd opened my mouth, was just about to ask who Pamela was, but Bonnie Jean'd reached out quick and pinched him—hard. And someone else, I didn't catch who, hissed, "Shaddup."

I asked anyway. "Who's Pamela?"

Silence. But a lot of movement. A lot of looking at anything but me. A little bit of shoe scraping. If this was a Warner Brothers cartoon, at least one of 'em would be whistling.

Besides the pushy kid, there was always the smart kid, the one who's got your number before you do. Bonnie Jean was that kid too. "You ain't the cops. Why you askin'? And how come you're up here anyways?"

All good questions.

"I'm a private detective. I came with the cops."

For that I was rewarded with a lot of big eyes and some happy gratified oooohs. Which is exactly how I would of reacted back when.

Before Bonnie Jean could stop him, the redhead was tugging at my sleeve, saying, "You betcha that's Pamela. She was bad. You gonna find out who kilt her?"

"I'm here to try. Bad? Why was she bad?"

Pushing him out of the way, Bonnie Jean was back in control. "Tell you one thing, Mr. Privates Defective," she said. "Ain't none of us gonna help you. Are we?" With that last crack, she gave the rest an eye as evil as Flo on her best day.

I knew the answer, but I had to ask anyway. "And why is that?"

"Because we gotta live here, and if you ever really did, you don't now."

4

I'd guess most of the kids who'd ever lived in the Home knew how to get up on the roof. I'd been out of this place since Bold Venture won the Kentucky Derby—when was that? fifteen, sixteen years?—but its secrets were still mine. They had to be. You spend your whole life in a neighborhood, a small town, a building big enough to house the New York Yankees, that place is yours. You know it better than you know yourself. Its secrets are your secrets. Especially if you're a kid like I was a kid, always poking around. Except for the queasy stomach when it came to slaughter, I was born to be a gumshoe. And one thing I knew now, knew as sure as I knew Mister had a recent hairpiece—the girl's name was Pamela and every kid in the Staten Island Home for Children knew who killed her. And why. I also knew not one of them was going to tell me.

All I had to do was know what they knew—which I was going to have to find out all by myself.

The roof was exactly as I remembered it. Aside from the towers, there was a whole lot of steeply angled tiled roofing a kid could kill himself sliding off. Up here there were four small areas of flat tar paper, each section set beside the four huge cone topped turrets. On these, in hot weather, you had to choose your way carefully or risk getting sticky black goo all over your shoes.

Shoes were hard to come by, harder to keep. A kid guarded his shoes.

The weather wasn't hot. It was cool and the tar was firm. But not all that firm. Up here there were footprints dating back to the Pleistocene. What I was looking for were footprints dating back a week, maybe even a week and a half ago. A week or so was just about enough time.

Sixty feet below, Lino, Mrs. Z, Mister, and entourage

were heading back into the house, leaving the guys who cleaned up to clean up. If I knew Lino, right about now he'd be thinking about having a look up on the roof, see if he could spot where the girl was pushed or got dropped or fell. By now, he might know her name and he might not. He might think of talking to the kids and he might not. But he was sure to be headed my way. I had maybe five minutes to myself.

Nothing but pigeon toes going every which way and seagull shit up here. No cigarette butts or spent matches. No scraps of torn clothing. Not even a bloody saw. The sound of Lino and Co. was getting louder. I needed to get farther out on the roof without messing with stuff already there. A plank would be perfect. There wasn't any plank. But there was an old window, left leaning against the bit of wall at the top of the ladder that ended at a door opening onto the roof. I grabbed it fast, set it down on the tarry roof and crawled out as far as I could go. No footprints. No handprints—wait a minute. There was the faintest pattern on the cool tar. I practically shoved my nose into it to get the best look. What was it? A board might show the grain of its wood. The window frame I was kneeling on might leave an imprint. It was material of some sort. What material would leave little crosshatched marks like these? And with that I remembered the blankets the kids were still using, old things, cheap things. I remembered the threadbare bedspreads. Called something—chenille? But oldest and cheapest of all were the sheets. What I was looking at was the imprint of a sheet. And here and there I was also looking at indentations made by knees or elbows or both. But not Pamela's knees or elbows. Even pregnant, Pamela was still a lightweight kid. These were made by someone heavier. And perhaps made even heavier by carrying a couple of someones smaller—like Pamela and her unborn babe. In the shallow indentations were little spots of dried blood. No doubt seeped through the sheet.

Later today some sort of cop would be up here scraping it off the tar paper and slipping flecks into an envelope. But not me. I needed a moment to think. None of the poor kids trapped below me had the strength to carry one of their own up the ladder to this roof, much less to crawl with her to its edge. And since it was impossible to spread out a sheet unless you could leave the body nearby while you did all this spreading, the sheet had to be here before any of that happened because there wasn't any "nearby."

The sheet proved planning and planning proved premeditation.

I had the old window propped up where I'd found it, and was back down the roof ladder and out of sight in a linen closet before Lino and his mob were climbing up it.

OK. There'd been a sheet spread out on a flat bit of roof, the bit that ended in the five-story drop into sumac. There wasn't a sheet there now. To have one ready and then to remove it had to mean the killer lived here, or at least worked here. Or—hell. I suddenly remembered all those wounded GIs down on the lower floors. Could it be some sick creep who'd knocked up a kid and then got rid of her?

I was out of the closet and down the stairs in seconds flat. In this game, I had to move fast. Lino was not only dumb, he jumped to conclusions faster than an incoming blockbuster.

It didn't take long to discover what should of been obvious. Any poor schlub bedded down in the Staten Island Home for Children was here for the long stay. As the beat cop said: none of 'em were going anywhere, least of all up a coupla flights of stairs to molest kids.

Now what? Scratch the burn victims in their jellied body bags. Forget the guys with half their heads blown off or those with missing limbs. Especially erase the sight of the piteous schnook with no arms *or* legs.

Since it had to be someone intact and also someone who worked here, that someone must know the place and where to get rid of the evidence. Who worked here? Kitchen staff. Cleaners. So it was down to the basement. Where better to get rid of a sheet and maybe a pair of pants with blood on the knees than the basement furnace? Little hope of finding anything like that, but some hope of finding something, anything, to help me out here.

Pulling the string that switched on the overhead bulb,

I found myself frozen, standing at the top of the narrow wooden stairs. I was staring, I was stuck in place, if I didn't get moving, I was lost.

The brick building with its four towers looked like Dracula's New York City address, but the basement looked like the Inquisition's tool shed. Always knew the Zawadzkis were bats, but this about beat all. Right below me had to be an altar. Over to the left was a confessional, no doubt about it. The rest of the space was filled up with me, several piles of varied scary junk, about seventy statues of JC plus friends.

And the furnace.

Took me awhile, but I finally got the furnace door open, one too small for an entire body to fit through—seemed logical that if one *could* of been, it *would* of been—when someone cleared his throat behind me. I must have jumped a foot straight up in the air.

When I got back down, I gasped, "Holy smoke, it's you. You spooked me."

Mister'd come out of the dark, one eye squinted like Popeye due to the smoke traveling up his narrow face from the butt stuck between his thin lips. "Work here."

"Of course you do."

"You don't."

"Never a truer word spoken."

"So whatchoo doin' here?"

"A stroll down memory lane?"

"Oh yeah? And whatchoo remember about the basement?"

"Aside from the shed where you used to listen to the radio, you were always down here."

"You got that right. Still do. Like the radio. Now I like Jack Benny most. And after him, I like *The Burns and Allen Show*."

"Makes sense. Gracie being dumb and all, and George being smart."

Mister gave me a cagey look. Was that an insult? A compliment? Since he didn't know and never would, he said, "You said it."

"Not a great day for the old school, Mister."

"Whatchoo mean?"

"A child killed."

Mister spat out the butt. It landed on the filthy cement floor and died there. "That one. That wasn't no child. Not no more."

"She was a child, Mister."

"Not in the eyes of God. And don't no one got bigger eyes than God."

"Excuse me, but what are you saying? You saying she had it coming?"

"Ain't sayin' nothin'."

I'd seen it before. Seen it over and over when I was growing up. Mister was getting hinky. And when Mister got hinky, us kids usually took a powder. The guy wasn't a gem at the best of times. At the worst of times, a kid didn't want to be anywhere near.

He was leaning over, picking something out of a pile of somethings, but his pale gooseberry eyes never left my face. He'd shut his mouth, but those eyes were still talking to me. They were saying: you bet she deserved it.

"You do it, Mister?"

"Do what?"

"Put her in the family way?"

Mister'd found what he'd been looking for, an old tire iron. Faster than I could get the gun out of my pocket, he'd swung at me hard as he could. Missed me by about a foot, but he was shouting so loud his spittle made it all the way to the sleeve of my favorite jacket. "Full of the Devil, that's you! That was always you whatever your real name is! You haven't even got a real name, nope, never. Me and Flo didn't even bother to give you one, not if God didn't. Bastard born and bred. Why I didn't send you back to Him when you was liddle, I'll never know. But you're goin' now!" And this time the tire iron was aimed at my head. It missed me only by inches. He wouldn't get another chance. I'd finally gotten my gun in my hand and had it pointed right between his eyes.

"Mister!"

Cringing in unison, Mister and I turned startled faces towards the basement stairs. Mrs. Z was standing there, hands clenched, muscles in her forearms bunched like cables. Behind her stood Lino. And behind him stood the comb-over beat cop with the moustache. Behind them could of been the Marx Brothers, we wouldn't have noticed. Flo was more than enough.

"You stop that right now, Mister! And you! Russo! Put the gat away. Where do you think you are?"

Suddenly meek as his savior's lamb, Mister dropped the iron. The clang it made hurt my teeth, not to mention my headache. Me, I slipped the "gat" back in my pocket.

Flo was across the gritty floor and had her arm around her husband's shoulders as fast as he could wield the iron. "Now, Mister, this ain't what we believe, is it?"

Without raising his eyes, his arms hanging slack at his sides, he said, "No. Don't."

"Look at me, Mister."

Mister raised his eyes to hers.

"What do we believe?"

"Only the ones God tells us."

"That's right. And who does God tell us needs doin'?"

"The bad ones. The ones He needs to start over with 'cause they came here all spoilt."

"That's right. That's good." Mister's eyes, still on hers, brightened. She asked him, "And if you were to take one God didn't tell you to take?"

"I'd be the bad one."

Right about here, Lino who'd been listening to this without expression, caught my eye. His own eye rolling, he said: "Blow me out a whale hole. It was Mister? He killed that poor child and her baby?"

Flo turned first to Lino and then to me, her gaze steady, her voice calm. "Mister has always done the cleaning up around here. Even the sheets. Good thing them sheets are cheap."

Listening, Lino lost his "heard it all before" deadpan. His face was like the sign at Times Square. Every little thought was running across it, round the back of his head, and right back across his face again. Gotta hand it to him though, his next question was clear enough. "And how long would that be, this 'cleaning up'?"

"Well, damn, Morelli. Whatchoo think? As long as me an' Mister've been here. Thirty years, year or two either side. Mister's never at a loss for something that needs cleaning up."

"And no one's ever noticed?"

"Why should they? Where you think you are? You oughta know these ain't kids anybody wants. One or two, even ten, go missin', who'd notice? If they ask, we tell 'em they ran away. 'Course, nobody asks."

"But the other children, don't they see?"

"Hah. In your day, wasn't as much to hide. But these days are bad days, right Mister?"

"Very bad."

"And them others know to keep their mouths shut. That right too, Mister?"

Mister, hangdog a moment ago, smiled. It wasn't pretty.

If Lino was like the Times Square sign, I was like the light bulbs at Coney Island. All lit at the same time, all different colors, and all flashing. What Bonnie Jean said, what she didn't say, it all made sense. The pictures I'd lived with growing up, they made sense. The kids I remember I'd see one day and not the next, they made sense too. Flooded with understanding, I tried to keep my own mouth shut— but it opened on its own and someone inside blurted out: "When I... when my mother got here, God was talking to you then?"

For that I was rewarded with one of Flo's arched eyebrows, as bushy as a Fuller brush. "God don't talk to me. He talks to Mister. And since you're gonna ask anyhoo, I'll answer you right now. That little slut came here to get rid of you, didn't she, Missssster Rooooso? Obvious as daylight. It was her gave my Mister the call. He knew soon as he saw that one getting shoved out of a po-lice car, her belly big with evil, oh yeah, he knew what his duty was. Right, Mister? That very night, what did you say to me?"

"I said God talked to me."

Flo reached out and grabbed Lino's checked tie. "Would God lie to a good man like Mister? God would not lie. So Mister did what he had to do. Buried her where all the others are now. In our wood. Mister calls it 'Good Riddance Acre'."

And with that, added to all my other sudden understanding—which was close to unbearable—came the deepest understanding I'd ever known. I understood the places in the woods we'd sometimes see, places we thought Mister was burying garbage. If I'd spoken right then, my voice would of been as high pitched as Caruso singing Mozart. The Maple Wood? Where I climbed trees? Built forts. Pretended I was Earle Sande bringing Zev home in 1923's Kentucky Derby or Gallant Fox in 1930? Where I got my first kiss and my first brush with a female breast? Our woods, the only place we ever felt free—all of us running oblivious over a graveyard.

My mother was just a kid in a jam. A kid nobody wanted or asked about. She hadn't left me here. She'd never missed me, never made it big somewhere. She'd never left at all.

I had to ask, throat as dry as Flo's heart. "Why not me too? Why not like the last one?"

"You?" For the first time, I was gifted with Mrs. Z's full regard. "Because you slithered out before Mister got to that little bitch. But that last one, the one you just found? You wanna know what a good man Mister is? He tried to save that baby. Tried to get it out of her. 'Cause it ain't the liddle one's fault, not really. Took 'em up to the roof, laid out a nice sheet so God's new life wouldn't get dirty, even used a clean saw. Show 'em your saw, Mister."

Mister reached behind the furnace and brought out a nice new hand saw. Cleaned and put neatly away. "My favorite," he said, as proud of the thing as London's Saucy Jack must have been proud of his knife.

Flo smiled at Mister and Mister smiled at Flo. True love was always touching.

But then the deep crease between Flo's blameless eyes got deeper. "But all he got for his trouble was a lot of stupid screaming from the slut, so he had to sock her one. It was all that blood made him stop. Mister's not used to too much blood. So he threw the whole mess off the roof. Must be why he left it lying there. The shock, you know." She leaned towards Lino. She did it so she could whisper, "Mister's getting forgetful these past few years." She shook her head, tears welling in the corners of her eyes. "Been thinking of getting him to see a doctor."

My head was throbbing, but I still heard myself say, "I hear good things about Bellevue."

Maybe someone heard me, maybe not. Didn't matter. Lino Morelli had solved a double murder case. On Staten Island, of all places.

I needed to get over to South Jersey. I might be just in time to catch the fifth at Monmouth Park. I had a tip on a horse that couldn't lose.

But most of all I needed a drink. Maybe a lot of them.

A week later, I was lying on a bed they would of used for kindling back when I was cannon fodder on the island of Luzon, along with the rest of the 26th Cavalry Regiment. The bed was in 4-A, the one room I called "home." From its single smeared window I could see exactly one tree in the Tompkinsville Park. Mostly I saw the dark brick building across Stapleton's Bay Street that was sure to have a guy just like me in a room just like mine. Only he wouldn't be reading my dog-eared copy of *The Bride Wore Black* because I was reading it. What he'd more likely be doing was watching television. I already hated television. Who could like television when they had a radio?

I was chain smoking; the fug in the room was dense enough to crash a plane in. The only other reading material within reach was a week old copy of the Staten Island *Advance* with a shot of Lino top of the fold. Morelli should of arrested the photographer for grievous facial rearrangement. He looked like something in the back of a special cage at the Bronx zoo.

I shouldn't of been chain smoking since about a buck fifty three was all that stood between me, a few more meals, a few more packs of Luckies, and the rent. Reading a book I'd read about five times already, I'd already reached the conclusion that the ciggies were more important than the rent—this cheap little room was giving me the Blues worse than listening to Billie Holiday on one of her sadder days. They all seemed to be sad to me, so sadder meant suicidal.

I was coming to the part in the book when Lew Wanger—my favorite thing, a detective—was beginning to realize what had seemed to the cops to be unrelated murders, were anything but, when the phone rang. A phone ringing in my room was about as unusual as a naked woman in my room

(times were dry in so many important ways) so could I help
it if I threw the book in the air, knocked the overflowing
ashtray off the edge of the end table, and stepped in the
reeking mess on the bare wood floor in my only clean pair
of socks?

What with all that, I still caught the call before the phone
stopped ringing.

"Yes? Hello? What?" I said this before I remembered I
was a PI and this was supposed to be an office phone. "Sam
Russo here. What can I do for you?"

"You're coming up to Saratoga."

"I am?"

"You the guy solved that murder on Staten Island?"

I glanced over at the *Advance* again. My name wasn't
mentioned. As usual.

"How——?"

Whoever was talking caught that one before I pitched it.
"Never mind. You that guy?"

"I am."

"Then you're the guy we want. There'll be a ticket
waiting for you at the ferry. It'll include a transfer to a train
out of Manhattan that'll take you all the way up here to
Saratoga Springs."

My heart did a double dip. Saratoga Springs was where
they kept the oldest and greatest race track in America. The
one that topped 'em all with the best jocks and the best horses
and the best... well, the best of everything you'd want if you
were like me, a horse racing fanatic.

The voice was still talking. "When you get to the Spa, I'll
be waiting for you. Show you where you'll be staying."

The "Spa." That's what insiders called it. And this guy
was telling me I'd be staying there.

"When's all this supposed to happen?"

"Right now."

"And who are you?"

"Doesn't matter."

"Does it matter why I'm doing all this?"

"Three dead jockeys enough for you?"

Christ on rye, hold the mayo, *one* dead jockey was enough

for me.

"I'm on my way."

"Of course you are."

The line went dead and I was standing there in ashy socks realizing I hadn't told the guy what I charged, I hadn't even found out if he was paying me. So what? I was going to Saratoga Springs in upstate New York and the season was only a few days old.

I was so surprised and excited, my legs gave a little. Good thing the bed was there or the rest of me would be covered in cigarette ash.

For me, any racetrack's home. Even a straight quarter mile plowed in the woods would do. Reading the racing forms, listening to the radio, I longed for Belmont. Pimlico. Monmouth. But especially the track at the Spa. I got myself to Monmouth as often as I could, to Belmont twice, Aqueduct maybe three times, but to Saratoga—I'd never once had enough folding green to get all the way up to Saratoga Springs.

This time all I needed was in the envelope that sure enough waited for me at my end of the Staten Island ferry.

Thanks to poor dead Pamela and her poor dead babe, someone was paying my way door to door.

It was one of those late July mornings when upstate New York makes you want to sing like Bing Crosby and drink like Tallulah Bankhead. Or drink like Bing and sing like Tallulah. Women's thin summer dresses weren't yet clinging to their legs like wet laundry and a guy's hat didn't slide to the back of his head.

It was the kind of day anyone with the nerve and the cash (not to mention luck and an honest tip-off) could make a bundle on the visions that flashed past on dirt or grass and made your blood pound with the glory of just one thing on this earth that was pure. To me, growing up with pigeons and rats and the Zawadzkis, plus enough cockroaches to sink the Staten Island ferry, a racehorse was all there was of beauty.

And there, waiting on the train platform, was the guy

who'd called me. An overfed guy in an expensive suit with
an expensive hat on his sleek head and expensive shoes on his
feet. But his face looked like a cheap Halloween mask out
of Stapleton's Five & Dime. He said his name was Marshall
Hutsell and stuck out his hand.

I shook it—even though I disliked him instantly. But
so? I didn't need to like him. Because of Marshall Hutsell,
or because of whoever Hutsell worked for, I wasn't hanging
around Lino's cop station with Lino's hand chosen bunch of
morons, all of 'em half hoping a call would come in about
something really gruesome, at the same time half hoping the
phone lines would go dead so they could finish their game of
Chinese checkers. Because of Hutsell and friends, my room
and board had been paid two weeks in advance for one of
the smaller suites in a pink hotel with pinker petunias in the
window boxes and a widow's walk way up at the top where
a widow, if she bothered to walk it, could see for miles. Pink
hotel and pink petunias were on a nice tree lined street called
Case Street, a block away from the entrance to Saratoga's
historic track.

I had a job, a hotel room with private bath and a pink
kitchenette, complete with a small stove, a small ice box,
some pots and pans, a set of dishes, and a set of cutlery right
down to the steak knives. I had entrée to the track at any
time, day or night, and some hard cash. That was in another
envelope Hutsell handed me right after delivering me to my
new home at the Spa.

An hour later I stood on holy ground—the backstretch
where only those in the game ever got to go.

Before this, the only time I ever saw a backstretch was
because of some trainer I knew. And all the trainers I knew
trained and raced claimers. Most were decent enough guys,
kept decent enough barns, and all their hot-walkers and
exercise kids and jocks on their way up or down were decent
enough too—for the most part. But barring a miracle, not
one of 'em was ever going to get that big horse. Like that big
case, the big horse was the stuff of dreams. But maybe Sam
Russo, Private Investigator, had a dream coming in. Why

not? It could happen to anyone.

I was not only in blue grass, I was in clover.

Marshall'd already told me nobody at the track actually knew for sure jocks were getting bumped off. At least nobody but whoever was doing the bumping. Basically the folks who hired me, faceless folks I hadn't yet met and maybe never would, were pretty much in the dark along with everyone else. Or so he said they said. No one was altogether certain it wasn't just a series of bad accidents—and for once not on the track—which is why they hadn't called the cops. Or, again, so he said they said. The cops agreed, which is why they hadn't shown up on their own. Or so they said.

Uh huh, is what I said to myself as I'd listened to all this horseshit, and I'm just like Dorothy Parker once said, the Queen of Romania. If three dead jocks one after another were accidents, three long shots had come in for Lady Coincidence.

But, like I said about coincidence, not one of them, maybe not even the cops, believed the accident angle for a minute.

That's what I was supposed to do. Help the guys who owned and ran and influenced the track believe it. Or help them chalk it up to a really bad streak of luck. The season was just starting. The war had shut things down for three long years. The big races Saratoga was used to hosting had gone off to Belmont. So did the customers all of Saratoga lived on. The last thing they needed was the money folk to stay away now the track was open again. Or even the penny ante bettor. Saratoga Springs was full of money all year round; it was that kind of place. But it could always use more; it was that kind of place too. Looking at a gaudy blood bay filly that must have cost someone more money than I'd ever see in my entire life, I thought: couldn't we all? I was no better than the town, and no worse. I could always use more.

As for the jockeys themselves, the ones not dead, you could describe them as a little spooked. Who wouldn't be? Deaths happened all the time on a racetrack, usually to the horses. An image of Dark Secret winning the '34 Jockey

Club Gold Cup with one broken leg rose up in my mind. I shut it down before I heard the "mercy shot" that killed him moments after he'd won someone a nice pot of money. But the jocks got crippled or killed every week at some track somewhere. Even so, it was an odd jockey who drowns in a Saratoga lake. Or one who, completely sober, crashes his car into a tree on an empty road at 4 a.m. Or, best for last, chokes on a ham sandwich at a picnic by a mineral springs consisting of just himself and his dog. The dog was one of those African dogs, the ones that don't bark. It also didn't leave its master's side. Hikers found them both a few days after the sad event.

And this had all happened in the space of nine days. One more like it, and if I'd been a jockey, I'd move me and my tack to Southern California. Fast.

8

So there I was, walking a shed row of the oldest and best looking track in the U.S. of A. remembering the last time I was at any track, Monmouth as usual, crammed up against the fence with the rest of the hoi polloi. I think my mouth was open. I think I was yelling. I think there was a fat guy next to me kissing his ticket over and over. I think he stank like a moose. I think I came this close to beaning him. I'd just lost my shirt on a sure thing in the second. Horse called Can't Beat Him. Funny thing is, everyone did, including the gate which they couldn't get him out of. The race went off and he was still in there trying to brain himself on the metal bars.

I did what the usual loser does; I threw my losing ticket away in disgust, all the time wondering if I was going to be spending the night in the city park, when a "stooper" came by to snatch it up, and I thought: Sam, things keep going like they're going, that'll be you in a month, stooping down to pick up discarded tickets hoping to find that little beauty thrown away by some idiot who couldn't read a winning number when they bought one.

But that was then and this was now and now I was on the backstretch with carte blanche to go where I liked. And I liked everywhere I could go. The tidy barns, newly painted. Horses, sleek as the finish on a new Packard, being led out to the track or led back. Horses dancing by on the track, getting a feel for it. Guys in cream colored suits and cream colored hats standing around staring at form sheets. Black kids, white kids, brown kids, old men, young women, forking straw into stalls or hosing down quivering hides. Farriers hammering shoes onto hooves or prying them off. The smell of it all. The sound of it all. Why do people keep trying to close down racetracks?

This is what I'd learned in my twenty seven years. God
in His Wisdom only talked to certain people and every one
of them was a first cousin to Groucho Marx who once said:
"Whatever it is, I'm against it."

Right about then, I spotted someone I knew: George
Labold. George Montgomery Labold was a jockeys' agent,
the first of his breed I'd ever met—this was back when I
was still a kid as well as still a detainee at Flo's place, not to
mention Mister's. Learned a lot from George and George's
friends for a whole three months one year, and got paid for
it by doing anything and everything he and his friends asked
me to. Worked my way up to exercising the horses. He was
the first guy who told me I could of made a hell of a jockey
if I weren't so big and bound to get bigger, and he oughta
know, being big himself, plus agenting a few of the good
ones in his time. I would of loved that, being a jockey. But
life doesn't work that way—getting what you love. Seemed
to me life gives you what you need. For most people, what
you loved wasn't on the table.

Anyhow, there was George and there I was, yelling hellos
at each other. Since he was half a foot taller, I was doing
my yelling upwards. At some point in all this, he asked me
what I was doing on the backstretch. It was for sure I hadn't
become a jockey. Was I rich? Was I an owner?

"Do I look rich to you, George?"

He looked me up and down. "Hard to tell these days.
You look like you seen a few things."

"We've all seen a few things."

"You mean with the war and all?"

"That's what I mean."

"Where'd you serve?"

"The Philippines."

"You mean Bataan and like that? Damn. Most of those
guys never made it back."

"I know."

And that's about all either of us wanted to say about the
war. He'd been too old to go and I was still too close from
coming back to want to remember too much.

"So if you ain't rich, why you here?"

"Dead jockeys."

From the way he just looked down on me, without a word, dead pan as Buster Keaton, I couldn't tell if he knew jocks were dying or not. George had come down a notch or two since I'd seen him last. The three who died probably weren't jocks he'd ever seen up close. They won too much, rode horses that competed in the big stakes.

Knowing how to ride thanks to George and his pals, plus how to care for horses, landed me in the Philippines. The U.S. had its last cavalry unit there, my regiment, the 26th. I'll never forget a single one of those horses, especially how it was when they got led away, eyes rolling in fear, to be butchered to feed the fellas who rode them against Japanese tanks and heavy artillery.

Those horses held the beach against the little guys with the big guns. For awhile.

A few of us, me included, never touched a single hair of their hide except to say goodbye. We could be starving, but we wouldn't, we couldn't, eat our horses.

Not another word out of George. He was already gone, off about his business which was collaring a trainer to get one of his jocks another mount. It was like the last time I saw him. That was the year Cavalcade won the Derby, the same year he was Horse of the Year. George's jocks never saw a Derby. But one or two of them saw a stakes race.

He had a good one once, a jockey out of South Carolina called Bingo Lance. Bingo died on the track along with the horse that was just about to win the Suburban Handicap.

That was one terrible day for horse and man and agent. Bingo was the closest he ever came to glory and the death of Bingo Lance was pretty much the death of George.

Standing with my hand out, I'd of liked to say more to George Labold, ask him to have a drink with me, maybe dinner in the pink hotel.

Hell, I was here for two weeks. I'd see him again.

Next thing I knew I was in another shed row looking at a mare called Gallorette.

I would of known her anywhere.

She was big and she was rangy and the year Hoop, Jr.

won the Kentucky Derby, Gallorette beat him. A few years back she was Champion Female Horse. This year, she was still knocking 'em over like bowling pins.

I made a fool of myself. I cooed at her. Called her darling. Dug out a handful of the peppermints I'd brought to the track and offered her a few. It was like making an offering to a goddess.

"Hey you! Get away from that horse! Who do you think you are?"

"Sam?"

"Are you nuts or something, Sam? This here's Gallorette and she's in the Whitney about an hour from now. You want her sick on sugar?"

I got away from her. Next to Gallorette, I wasn't anyone. Just a lonely PI in paradise. One where jocks were getting killed.

9

My life was measured out by Kentucky Derby winners. World events, women, jobs, places I'd been—none of 'em counted as markers.

I told time by the Derby.

I wish I could say I was born the year Man 'O War won, but since he didn't start in the big race, I couldn't. A horse called Paul Jones won. I'd tried hard not to be bitter, but being born in the year of Paul Jones got my goat. I made up for it a little bit by my first escape from the Staten Island Home for Hopeless Kiddies. That was the year Reigh Count came home with ease. Lino and me, we got dragged back when the Count took the Saratoga Cup.

We spent those few months on the streets of New York City with some newsies, sleeping in alleys under cardboard, eating out of trash cans, learning how to choose the right mark and boost a wallet or two. We learned how to roll a drunk. But nicely. I've always had a nice way about me. Lino wasn't so nice, but being a cop at heart, he felt guilty. Sometimes he'd take the money but find a way to get the wallet and all its pictures and cards and stuff back to its owner.

I discovered girls the year Brokers Tip took home the roses. What a race. The two leading jockeys, Meade on Brokers Tip and Fisher on Head Play, punched each other all the way down the backstretch and across the finish line. As a kid, I loved it. Hey. I loved it now. I also loved Rosemarie for about three months.

I learned a lot from Rosie. She learned nothing from me, but she was real sweet about it. She wasn't so sweet when I went off with Ellen. And then Ellen didn't like Corrie. Corrie paid her brother to beat me up when I met Angela. That was a banner year for girls.

In Omaha's big year, all on my lonesome, I made it out of that place they called a home. I got all the way to Monmouth Park, hitchhiking, hopping trains. They didn't find me for months. During those months I haunted the barns meeting George Montgomery Labold and George's pals. One of 'em was a claiming trainer, training horses at the bottom end of Thoroughbred horse racing. Even so, from Carl—claiming trainer's name was Carl Hessing—I'd learned enough so I got to get up on a glossy back now and then to exercise some better horses than Carl's horses, high bred nags that took a stakes race now and then. Someone must have snitched. Only way Mister Zawadzki could find me and haul me "home" in his Model T dump truck.

Thinking back, that was the time of my life.

Why would Mister and Mrs. Z want me back? Because the Zawadskis were paid by the head and every once in a while someone came counting heads. (As for those missing, Mrs. Z'd already made that one easy, even for Lino. Few asked and when they actually did, they got the same answer: little sonofabitch ran away, din't he? Or din't she? Until Pamela, it always worked because one or the other of us was always trying to run away.)

My final escape from the ancestral home was with Bold Venture. We weren't world beaters, that horse and me, but we were survivors. It was a lucky year for horse and boy; our competition was preoccupied with jam ups and getting knocked to its knees. This meant clear sailing ahead for us and we both grabbed the advantage. Bold Venture took the Derby. And I took nothing since I had nothing but the clothes I stood up in. If Flo and Mister noticed I was gone, the way the times were, it was for sure they were happy to see the back of me. Was I happy? You bet. I whistled all the way off the Island of Staten. I already knew how to sleep rough and how to sell newspapers. I knew how to groom and exercise race horses.

I was on my way until the war showed up.

1941. That was Whirlaway's year. And we both did. Whirl away. Him to fame and glory; me to gore and horror in the Philippines and a crash course in scraping the bottom of human nature.

But all that was history. The war was over. Hitler and Goebbels and Himmler were wherever people like Himmler and Goebbels and Hitler go. The Japanese were back where they belonged, in Japan. The Philippines were once again ours. Though we stole it from the Spanish who'd stolen it from the— oh, the hell with it, this kind of thing went on as far back as men could grunt. I hoped I was over Carole Lombard's fatal plane crash into the side of a mountain. Gable wasn't.

I didn't suppose I was either, not completely. I didn't think I'd ever be.

But here I was in Saratoga, Citation had just won the Derby and the Preakness and the Belmont, the great Gallorette won the Whitney right in front of me, her long lean chestnut body flattened out and flying, and I was just about to embark on my first serious case, one that was all mine, no Lino, one I might actually solve. To be honest, the idea that I'd succeed did not loom large in my innermost heart. Even so, I had a job, one that did not include shoplifters or grifters or people cheating on their better halves.

I'd been hired by men who thought I was a real PI.

What I didn't have was a single idea about how to begin.

In *The Maltese Falcon*, Bogie was a seasoned PI with a partner and an office and a gun and a window with his name painted on it. A couple of years ago, I saw a movie at the Paramount four times on four consecutive nights, a real humdinger of a picture called *The Big Sleep*. In it, Bogie was still a PI, but this time without a partner. Even so, he still had a gun and an office that had a window with his name on it. Different name, but same idea. Me? I had that room on Staten Island which was no place to have a room, a pot bellied stove I used for heat in the winter, a stained sink, a toothbrush, some business cards in the back of a bureau drawer, and a snub nosed Colt .38 Detective's Special. The snubbie was a belly gun, easy to conceal, easy to use in a hurry. I knew about using guns thanks to using a variety of them against a lot of little people shooting at me or strafing me or lobbing bombs at me. I had the chutzpah to take on a job I didn't have the first idea about. But I could read. That helped. And Saratoga had a fine little library. That helped too.

But what helped most of all was the privilege of watching a great mare named Gallorette take the Whitney Stakes from a field of outclassed males.

I spent the next two days "on the job" reading Agatha Christie and Raymond Chandler. For comic relief, I snuck in something newly minted called *1984*.

On the third day, I was ready for anything.

Good thing no one died while I was boning up on what to do about it.

10

I made coffee in my little pink kitchenette. I poured a slug of some good stuff in the coffee. I sat in a white whicker rocking chair on the pink front porch of my pink hotel and rocked and sipped and smoked and thought about why anyone would want to kill jockeys. One jockey made sense. I could come up with a dozen reasons for one dead jock. Saratoga was loaded with gambling joints, a few for the upper crust, most of 'em for the rest of us. Some were out there for all to see. The rest were tucked away in tucked away places which meant you had to go looking for 'em. So maybe the jockey owed someone bad some serious money. Or maybe he wouldn't throw a race. Then there was always the one where a jock knew too much about the kind of hoods who could fix anything that could be fixed— like back when Rothstein fixed the 1919 World Series and probably fixed the 1921 running of the Travers. Or maybe an owner or a trainer found out he was dirty and lost them a high paying Grade I stakes race. It could even be chalked up to a real accident, like the disappearance of Citation's rider, Al Snider. A few months back, Snider and a couple of his buddies disappeared off a fishing skiff near the Florida Everglades. It was dusk and a storm was building. The skiff was found but not Snider.

Al was one year older than me. He was headed to the top of his game. A few months later, Citation won the Derby. He won the Preakness and the Belmont. It was Al Snider who should of been in those winner's circles.

There was also the possibility that the guy's wife did it. I could think of a dozen reasons for *that*.

But *three* jockeys?

I spent over an hour in the Saratoga sun doing what Hercule Poirot liked to do, think, but Poirot was English—

sorry, Belgian.

I was wearing dark glasses. Poirot wouldn't wear sunglasses. But Philip Marlowe would.

No getting round it. Time to do what the red-blooded American Philip Marlowe would do. Wear the dark glasses. Get to the track. Buttonhole a few people. Ask 'em questions. Talk about the jockeys. Find the connection between them. There had to be a connection.

I heard Bogie say, "What's keeping you, kid?"

I said, "I'm moving, I'm moving, I'm off my rocker."

I'd walk across Congress Park, look at a few horses in a few stalls, find the jockey's room, talk to a couple of 'em. One or two had to know something.

Scratch that idea, Russo. Talking to jockeys when they're suiting up for the day's meet wasn't the smartest idea. First off, it's hard to talk to a man with his head down a toilet. Half of 'em would be puking up just one more ounce to make weight. Second, if they weren't puking they'd be listening to a trainer. Third, I wasn't supposed to be doing any detecting here. What I was really here for was not to stir up a wasp's nest of cops and press and panicked tourists. I sure wasn't supposed to spook the jocks.

Here's what I was being paid for. A few weeks of soft Saratoga living, filled with the flash and dash of the best racing had to offer. After that I'd present a report stating that in each case it was a lamentable accident. For all I knew, it could be true. They could be accidents. Stranger things had happened. I didn't know many, if any, but a hundred to one they had.

I'd been hired to prove they were accidents. Or at least *not* prove anything else.

I didn't like it. It smelled like selling out. Would Bogie do it? The real question was: would Sam Russo do it?

You'd think I'd know the answer to that. I didn't. I was in Saratoga Springs. I was near the best racehorses in America. I was sleeping on a soft bed. I had an expense account. I was being tested.

Maybe in a day or two I'd know my answer. In a day or two I'd know who Sam Russo really was. For now, all I had was hope.

Dressed as any one of a thousand swells come to town for the season, still wearing the dark glasses, I made my way to the newspaper office. I thought the local rag would know a thing or two they hadn't printed. Well, that was the idea anyway. But why they'd tell me was something I was working out as I strolled south along Broadway.

"Sam! Hey, Russo!"

I froze. Christ on a hamburger bun. Who the hell did I know in Saratoga besides George Labold? Worse, who the hell knew me? I turned. Slowly. No pretending I hadn't heard the voice. No use running.

I didn't even know the guy's name. But I knew his face. It was that barely grown-up lug, the one with a comb-over, the tongue-depressor-moustache and boozer's breath.

Why would a Staten Island cop, the one guarding poor little Pamela's crime scene, be in Saratoga when I was in Saratoga? (Speaking of Lino's latest case, I'd learned Pamela's last name was Teager, that she'd been raped by her uncle, the wonderful Rudy Teager, and that her loving father took his brother in, but threw Pamela out. After that, somehow she'd made her way to the Staten Island Home for Children, where Mister—acting for his merciful God—put her out of his misery.) Here, in all his rooty toot zoot-suited glory stood the kewpie-doll cop. I was exaggerating. What he was wearing was not a Zoot suit. But it could of been. The bright green material was shiny enough and green enough and too big enough.

I slipped off the glasses to check I was seeing what I was seeing.

If he noticed me doing that, I couldn't tell. He had his hand out. I was supposed to shake it—in public, where decently dressed citizens could see me doing it. It was embarrassing. So I put out my own hand hard enough to propel him into the nearest half private place—which happened to be a bar called *The Finish Line*.

He minded getting shoved into a bar—with a name, I thought, that summed up drinking to a T—about as much as I minded sitting through a Bogart double feature. Not that I minded drinking. I liked drinking. But not before noon. Most people drew a line somewhere. Seemed this guy didn't know how to draw. Now I was closer, I could smell his choice of poison: Old Crow. He and his suit were "aged" in the stuff. I'd noticed it back in Stapleton standing around Pamela and her crime scene.

A smell strong enough to compete with all that was some smell.

"You buying me a drink, Russo?"

I didn't have an answer to that one. Dragging him into *The Finish Line*, I'd acted on instinct alone. So I bought him a drink. I asked for a glass of water. On the rocks. I got a glass of water without ice and a funny look from the barman.

"Thanks," said whoever this cop was, knocking back my gift with one quick bend of his wrist. "Never thought I'd see you up here. Figured you for a strictly Monmouth Park kind of guy. You wanna know why I'm up here?"

No. Yes. No. Well actually yes. "You came for the mineral waters?"

"Hah! Nah. I came 'cause your old pal Lino fired me. So I'm not a flatfoot no more. Boo hoo. But about two hours later this other guy hired me."

The hair on the back of my neck crisped a little at that. "Oh yeah?" I wanted to ask why Lino fired him. I wanted to ask why anyone else would hire him. I wanted to know what he was hired *for*. Did it have anything to do with dead jockeys? I didn't say a thing besides "Oh yeah?"

"I'm standing there, looking at nothing, right? And I mean nothing. It's out of the blue, what Lino done. And I'm a vet like you and about a million other guys and I've just lost about the seventeenth job in a row, and this guy walks up and he says, you look like you could use a little work. And I say, you ain't just whistling Dixie. And he says, well then, giddyap, pal, 'cause you're perfect for this job I got. So I get into this car— "

"Hold on. You just got into a car?"

"Sure. Who wouldn't get into a brand new Cadillac?"

"About everyone I can think of," I said, "unless there's a gun involved."

I don't think he heard me. He was still waxing lyrical. He'd also ordered another Old Crow—on my dime. And this was a guy I didn't even know the name of, and didn't hope to find out. All I was doing by now was wondering if there was a back door to *The Finish Line*, one by the men's room, and if I went out it, would I still be headed in the right direction for the offices of *The Saratogian*? Now there's a name you don't get to say too much—unless you live in Saratoga. Or as I've said they say up here: the Spa.

"So guess what the job is? Say barman, you wanna pour me another? And top him up too."

This made them both laugh so hard—the idea a man would drink water when he could be knocking back watered down hootch—they doubled over, and I was headed for the men's room.

My new friend, the ex-flatfoot, straightened up, coughing. "Wait! I haven't told you what the job is."

I had to know. So I stopped. "OK. What's the job?"

"Day off today, but usually I'm track security. Don't that beat all? I get paid to wander around the Saratoga racetrack inna uniform checking people ain't sneakin' in and keepin' an eye out for pickpockets."

"Lucky you. So you saw Gallorette win the Whitney?"

"Who? What?"

"A great horse in a great race."

"Oh yeah?"

"Yeah. Right now I gotta see a guy about a tree."

11

I was out the back door, around a corner, and up an alley fast, then quickly across Congress Street where I did a kind of first base slide into a lot full of parked cars. Me and the cars were all behind the biggest hotel I'd ever seen. The "lot" had to of been the stable yard where the guests of a hotel big enough to house Versailles, and all its wigs, once kept their fine carriages and fine horses—but now kept their cars. And what cars. It was a glittering metallic sea of snazzy cars. A brand new Cadillac wouldn't merit a second glance.

Forget the hotel. Who cared about a hotel full of swells? I was supposed to be working here. So far all I'd done was read library books and buy an idiot in a green suit a couple of cheap shots of Old Crow.

Out of the parking lot and down the street I found the newspaper office. It was a nice place for a mostly nice town, and there I read a two week old newspaper report on the accidental drowning of Manny Walker. Walker'd been twenty years old, a native of Troy, New York, a professional jockey for two years, and moving up fast in the riding stats. In fact, one more win and he'd of topped the list. This was mostly due to his getting the ride on Fleeting Fancy, this year's sensational three-year-old filly, another female up against the boys in Saratoga's Mid-Summer Derby, aka the Travers Stakes. Paper said the official cause was drowning by accident while swimming. As Walker was known to keep in shape by swimming before a day's races (he was found by some old guy named Herb Bedwell out rowing around looking for a place to do some quiet early morning fishing), the fact of his being alone, not five feet from the lake's small dock, face down in the water weeds with a snapping turtle waiting to sun itself on his cold dead back, surprised no one. There'd been some talk of how a lad so fit and so able could drown at all, but these things could happen to anyone. Especially the water weeds part. Even the best swimmer, once tangled up in that stuff, could get into trouble. And I oughta know; I got stuck once myself. Good old Lino Morelli pulled me out. He was also the one pushed me in.

Two days later, *The Saratogian* was writing about Matthew Mark McBartle. McBartle, born in Scottsboro, Alabama, won two graded stakes in one day at Belmont, was among the top three winning riders at Atlantic City Race Track, and like every other top American jock, showed up in Saratoga for its short rich season of racing. McBartle had the mount on Court'n Spark, a highly regarded entry in the upcoming Travers Stakes.

For reasons unknown, M. M. McBartle had gone for a spin in his brand new Mercury convertible in the middle of the night. He was twenty one years old, he'd been alone, had not been drinking, had not been out earlier with the boys, and from all accounts was up in his room at the Grand Union by 9 p.m. Hours later, he got up, got dressed, and went out. He left the hotel at 3:15 a.m. exactly. The time was noted by the night elevator operator. A short while later, on a small country road headed north to Glens Falls, his sleek little convertible slammed into a huge sycamore tree. Both car and driver were write-offs. There were no skid marks, no other cars on the road, no house nearby, no dead deer, mangled moose, crushed caribou or deranged dog he might have tried to avoid. There was nothing but a dead jockey. The police concluded that young McBartle had fallen asleep at the wheel. Verdict: automobile accident.

The last death happened only two days before my arrival, which was one day before the guy who knew some guys made a long distance call all the way to Stapleton, Staten Island, to hire me to make sure the police had got it right.

The third kid was 17, was raised in the stables of one of the flashier Lexington, Kentucky, horse farms, and before he died was running neck and neck with Manny Walker for top honors at Belmont. Babe Duffy, Manny Walker and Matthew Mark McBartle were all three trying to outride each other at Saratoga's short meet before each met his "accident."

The last, Babe Duffy and his barkless dog, Jane, had hiked out to one of Saratoga's mineral springs—when the wind was just right, the whole city stank of 'em—and sat himself down on a nice shiny rock. The paper assumed he was there for a picnic. Some picnic, his ham sandwich went down the wrong way, or wouldn't go down at all, or something, and with Jane helpless beside him, he died of asphyxiation. Slumped there, his hands clutching his swollen neck, his face the color of a ripe eggplant, a couple of tourists stumbled over them. It took a trained member of the local pound to get past Duffy's dog Jane so they could take the body away.

For the third time, the verdict was accidental death.

Babe Duffy was the regular rider of Hornet's Nest, a flashy grey gelding who was on a roll: eight solid wins at three different tracks. Hornet's Nest was also a Travers entry.

All three were young, all three were promising first rate jockeys, all three died within a little over a week of each other during the Saratoga season, all three had mounts in the Travers—and all three were accidents.

Right. If that was true, and I had to admit it could be, Lino Morelli understood the Theory of Relativity.

12

She was everything I thought she'd be. Tall, sleek, legs that wouldn't stop, enormous soft eyes that didn't miss a trick. Dark glasses pushed up on my head, I first saw her standing in the morning sun like a Lincoln penny fresh from the mint. She was looking at me just like I was looking at her. But what she had to be seeing wasn't a patch on what I was seeing. I was looking at years of breeding. I was looking at dreams come true. I was looking at a million bucks. She was looking at a guy who was piecing his life together from books he'd read and movies he'd seen. A guy who thought the shadows on a big screen were talking to him. Why she was looking at me, I couldn't say. If I were her, I wouldn't be. But she was. Both of us were staring like what we were seeing was all there was in the world to see.

She broke the spell first. I could of kept it up for hours. But when she did, I finally noticed that the woman who stood at her perfect head, a slender brown leather gloved hand holding her halter, wasn't half bad either.

The big difference was in the eyes. Fleeting Fancy's eyes were honest and kind. You couldn't say the same for Mrs. Willingford, third wife of old man "Joker" Willingford, fourth generation owner of one of Kentucky's biggest distilleries (*Joker's Special Blend*), fourth generation breeder of some of Kentucky's best horseflesh, and owner as well of the venerable Beeswing Farm. He'd also bred and still owned Fleeting Fancy, the glorious three-year-old filly who'd won everything a two- and three-year-old filly could win. The only two fillies came close to her were Honeymoon, but Honeymoon was cleaning up out in California, missing—or avoiding—the big Eastern races. And then there was Gallorette. Gallorette, at age 4, was certainly the bee's knees. She was also here in Saratoga having just beaten the

boys—again—in the Whitney. Racing in stakes events open
to both male and female horses was the only way to make
good money with a great female since the races restricted to
fillies and mares offered smaller purses. Same thing went for
the up and coming Fleeting Fancy. That is, it would be soon
as they found Fancy another jockey, one at least as good as
Manny Walker was turning out to be. Going on two weeks
since the kid'd met with his swimming accident and neither
Scratch Mason, the Willingford's trainer (so named because
he'd scratch a horse for a puddle on the track or three crows
on a railing), or the Willingfords themselves had come up
with a replacement.

The old guys standing over by the fence, the ones who
never placed a bet before having a good look at the horse,
top, bottom and sideways, were saying Fancy's people had
seen every jock from here to Paris. No one was taking
chances her new jock would get her beat.

I'd seen Gallorette. Gallorette was something to see.
But Fleeting Fancy. There was just something about her,
something I'd never seen in a horse before. The look in her
eye. The arch of her neck. The way she used her feet, like a
dancer. I couldn't imagine anything beating her.

Getting back to eyes, Mrs. Willingford had a pair like a
famous old nag called Boston. I'd always liked the sound of
Boston. I wish I'd met him. I didn't think I'd like meeting
Mrs. Willingford. Her baby blues didn't miss a trick, but
what the eyes didn't miss, her perfect California teeth
looked like they wanted to bite. She was as like Boston as
Boston'd been. Boston bit. Boston kicked. Boston bucked.
Boston raised a hell of a fuss. To tame the beast, for a whole
year, his trainer turned him into a hack between the traces
of a cab. It worked, but only well enough to race him. He
still bit man and beast, kicked anything got near enough, and
until the day he died raised a racket all by himself in his own
stall. Mrs. Willingford was smart enough to know all that
wouldn't work for her, not half as well as cunning. That was
what I saw in her eyes: more cunning than Flo Zawadzki ever
dredged up.

Looking at Joker Willingford's wife, in the back of my

head I heard Brigid O'Shaughnessy playing Sam Spade within an inch of his life. She said, "I haven't lived a good life. I've been bad. Worse than you could know."

Spade bought it. But when push came to shove, he turned her in at the end. Would I of done the same? Getting an eyeful of Mrs. Willingford, she was everything money could buy. Which, no matter what wise guys and philosophers say, was quite a lot. So yes, no, yes—honestly, I didn't know. All I knew was sometimes my imagination got the best of me.

Like Fleeting Fancy had stared, Mrs. Willingford was staring at me. I looked both sides, no one was standing near. I looked behind me. No one there either. Sam Russo wasn't a world beater when it came to looks, but I wasn't too bad either. I'd had my share of the finer females. Nothing had stuck. So far, it was me who didn't do the sticking because so far it wasn't worth the trouble a woman brought a man. Speaking of trouble, that's what Mrs. Willingford looked like—a beautiful blonde bundle of bother. In other words, trouble. Alluring trouble, true, but the kind of trouble it didn't pay a guy to mess with.

That Mrs. Willingford (first name Lois, but known to most as Mrs. Willingford—I knew because I'd asked around about the owners of Fleeting Fancy) was also getting an eyeful of me didn't make me bolt for cover. What did surprise me was how open she was about it. Like I was in a sales ring with a number slapped on my rump.

Standing next to both filly and woman was a kid could pass for maybe fourteen, but I knew he had to be sixteen at least. Looked like a bug boy, but he'd paid his dues, he was a working jockey, no question about it.

The kid was looking at Fleeting Fancy like she was the second coming—which for someone like him starting out in the game, she was. Fleeting Fancy could make him a star in one race. That is, if he could get the mount. Days and days of looking for a jock by Scratch and the Willingfords, he probably thought maybe they were getting a little desperate. And they probably were. My guess was this kid was hoping they'd be desperate enough to pick him.

I asked a guy by the fence if he knew the kid's name.

Nothing doing. I asked another guy. It took a few more guys before someone could name the kid we were looking at. He was Toby Tyrrell all the way from some Podunk dump in Florida. To the railbirds, Tyrrell was another kid with loads of promise like Manny Walker, Matthew Mark McBartle and Babe Duffy. Only difference was, he hadn't won anything worth getting excited about.

"I seen him race," said a fellow who probably had two eyes. It was hard to tell under more eyebrows than most men had hair. "Down in Florida. Hialeah to be exact."

"And?" That's the question I would of asked if his friend hadn't beat me to it.

"Just an overnighter," he said, "but I tell ya, the kid's got hands on him like George Woolf."

"G'wan. He's just a boy."

"I seen the Iceman ride. I know what I'm sayin'."

At this, every eye in every head had another look at Toby Tyrrell. Including mine. Which meant I was looking at an eager hopeful kid and didn't notice until I could smell her scent that Mrs. Willingford was holding out a cigarette (hers was already lit, its end blooded with red lipstick) offering it to me.

As I took it, she leaned in close, clogging my nose with heavy scent. "You like it? It's called *L'air du Temps*. No one has it yet but me. Joker bought me a crateful." And then in a deep brown voice she said, "You look like someone who needs to relax."

I took the cigarette. I let her light it for me. If I hadn't, would things have happened the way they did? Who knows? Another thing I've learned: the universe is full of surprises— and not all of them get a man where he wants to go. Of course, it's a rare man who knows where he wants to go. He just thinks he does. Not the same thing at all.

I thought I wanted to go where Mrs. Willingford was willing to take me.

13

We took her car. Sitting on the caramel colored leather passenger seat, watching the scenery go by, I told myself I was working the case. What I didn't tell myself was how. It didn't matter. There's this thing about us men. Where a fine looking woman is concerned, even a smart guy's brains ooze out his ears.

She was driving, and driving fast, along a little back road headed north. I didn't need a map to know it was the same road Matthew Mark McBartle took the night he died.

About two miles out of town, Mrs. Willingford pointed a long red fingernail towards an enormous tree coming at us at speed. "There. That's the tree that poor boy hit."

"Or vice versa," I muttered, looking. Who wouldn't look? There's something about where a person dies. It becomes special somehow. Holy? Unholy? Unlucky? Fated? Forever theirs? I could go on and on like that. But I gave it up and just stared for as long as I could. First straight ahead, then to the side, then with my head turned as far as it would go as the tree disappeared around a bend in the road.

Obviously, McBartle and his Mercury got the worst of it. The tree had a raw chunk taken out, some bark scattered around, but was otherwise going to live.

We wound up at some bar a mile farther along the narrow country road. With what was left of my brains, pickled as they were in gardenia and musk, I wondered if the bar was where McBartle was headed for when he took that last wrong unbraked turn.

Haven's Inn looked like my idea of where Hansel and Gretel wound up. I don't know what it looked like to Mrs. Willingford, but she was obviously no stranger there. We were escorted by the owner himself directly to a booth by a big back window, one that showed us a lot more trees. There was a glint of blue shining off in the distance.

"Lake," said the owner, a tall thin number with more teeth than I was used to in one mouth. "Not *that* lake."

For a minute, I didn't catch on. Which he noticed.

"Not the lake where the jock got his."

"Oh, right."

"*That* lake is near the track. *This* lake has cabins."

I didn't need another word to know Mrs. Willingford knew as much about the cabins back through the trees as the owner did. No doubt she spent more time in one or the other of them than he ever would.

The moment he'd left with our order—I should say hers, since she'd ordered sidecars for both of us—she reached over with both hands to hold just one of mine. I didn't move. It didn't seem polite. Besides, my brains were still down around my groin somewhere. "You have to stop calling me Mrs. Willingford."

"I like Mrs. Willing… ford. It suits you."

She threw back her head and laughed. I had to give it to her. Her long white throat was as good looking as the rest of her. And her laughter was infectious. It was all I could do not to laugh along. It helped that one of us didn't know what we'd be laughing about. She lowered her head, looked me right in the eye, and said, "I want you to call me something else."

"Far as I've heard, no one calls you something else. Except maybe Mr. Willingford. If I were Mr. Willingford, I'd think twice about even calling you Mrs."

Just about to do the laughing routine again, she changed her mind. She even let go of my hand. "I wonder if this is a mistake."

"Probably."

"I'm not used to men with brains."

"Believe me, if I had brains, I wouldn't be here."

"I find that insulting."

"I find it embarrassing. A man likes to think he's in control."

"And you're not?"

"Not in the slightest."

She put her hands back on my mine again. I hadn't moved it. Not even when the sidecars arrived. "I didn't expect you to be cute."

I'd heard a line like that line before. In a movie without Mary Astor. It'd been addressed to Bogie by the fruitcake half of one of two sisters, the half who turned out to be a killer. Did I think Mrs. Willingford was a killer? Certainly. But not the kind that left dead bodies—just dead hearts.

"What did you expect?"

"From a lowly shamus?"

Interesting. Like I knew this and that about her, she knew this and that about me. I'll bet she also knew who'd hired me and why. I'd even make bet she was one of those who did the hiring. Her or her hubby or both. "Even a lowly shamus has standards."

She looked like she wasn't sure if she was offended—again. While she was working that out, I sipped at my sidecar (whoa, Mrs. Willingford must be the owner's best customer, no stinting on the cognac), and had a look at the rest of *Haven's Inn*. The part I liked best was the lack of dead deer heads glued to the pine walls. Not even a moose over the huge stone fireplace. What I liked even better was the friendly face grinning at me from a barstool.

Paul Jarrett was not only a hard working jockeys' agent as well as one of the funniest guys I ever knew, plus about the best looking, he was also an alumni of my old alma mater, the Staten Island Home for Children.

If anyone was going to break Mrs. Willingford's spell, it was Jarrett—even wearing a Hawaiian shirt. The shirt was purple and covered with enormous yellow flowers. No one but Paul would wear it. No one but Paul had the gumption. Or the bad taste. Whichever.

"You keep chewing on that until I get back," I told her, "I can't miss this."

14

First thing Paul said to me, after the bear hug (he'd been a strong kid though only an inch or so taller than me; he was now a strong guy, not an ounce of fat on him, solid muscle—practically lifted me off my feet), was, "Heard about Mister. Not surprised in the least. But sorry to hear about your mom. That was bad. Real bad."

"I've filed it, Paul. Way down, deep as it goes."

"Understood."

I turned my glass round and round in my hands. "And there we were, thinking the words 'Staten Island' and 'murder' didn't go together."

Paul stared at me. "You kiddin', kiddo?"

"Not that I'm aware of."

"Well, think again. You ever hear of Albert Fish?"

"*The* Albert Fish? The Brooklyn Vampire? The Gray Man who killed and tortured who knows how many children and ate their—"

"Well I ain't talkin' about my Mom's pet guppy. And you're all grown up now. You can say 'butts.'"

Once again, he'd made me smile, not that Fish was funny. But Paul just had that way about him. "OK, go on. Tell me about how the island and Albert Fish go together."

Paul leaned closer over the table. He used to do that exact same thing after lights were out and he'd tell us all ghost stories. He could tell a story, any story, so well we'd all spend hours shivering under our meager covers. "Once they finally caught him, '35 I think it was, he boasted he'd killed or raped or tortured over a hundred little kids. And one of 'em was a poor little eight year old boy he'd seen playin' on his front porch in Port Richmond."

"Our Port Richmond!"

"The very one. They found the kid later in the woods

strangled with his own suspenders. That was in '24 or '25."

"Seriously?"

"The police sure thought so and it's a safe bet that Francis X. McDonnell's mom and dad thought so."

"If I'm so smart, how come I didn't know that?"

"Some of us knew some things when we were kids, and some of us knew other things. Mister told me about Fish."

"Why the hell would he tell you that?"

"To scare me? To keep me in line. Who knows about Mister? He could surprise a kid. He sure surprised you."

"That he did."

Paul peeked over my shoulder. "As for me, I *am* surprised about Mrs. Willingford over there."

"What? I'm not good enough for her?"

"Too good. Be careful. She gets her nose out of joint, guys like us get other stuff out of joint."

"Point taken. Which means I can't hang around here too long. Look. I'm staying at the Pascal House on Case Street."

"Pink suits you."

I let that one go right on by. "You got some time to come round and talk over old times?"

"You bet. Am I hearing you got an actual case?"

"Amazingly enough, yes."

"I'll come tonight. You can tell me about it."

"Eight o'clock?"

"Eight it is. That's if you can escape the clutches of the Joker's wild card."

I snuck a look. Mrs. Willingford was inspecting her make-up in a small blue enameled compact. A smaller pink tongue licked something off her painted lips. I remembered something I'd only been reading a few days back. Something out of *The Bride Wore Black*. "...those ice-cold eyes, that kissable mouth."

I said: "She's not Lombard."

"Nobody is."

I gave him one of my best smiles. He caught it and gave it back.

"That shirt suits you."

He looked down at it and laughed. "Couldn't resist it. Bet you wish you had one."

"You'd lose."

I'd always liked Paul. Admired him. Followed him around in the woods playing Cowboys and Indians. Cribbed from his math papers. He was better at that stuff than me. Though I beat him all hollow at reading. He wasn't much of a reader. When it came to books, I was school champ. But when it came to figuring out things to get up to in the middle of the night, Paul was our man. That he ended up a jocks' agent was a bit of a stumper. Being locked up in the Kid's Joint, it was hard for us kids to learn any kind of skill. So where he'd caught the racing bug had to be from me. I figured he was an agent for the same reason I was a PI. Both due to our being too big to be jockeys. We were like the guys who had a lot of friends who were musicians, but we couldn't play anything, not even a kazoo, and we couldn't sing a note, so we ended up managing the band. I thought he was that guy just like I'd of been that guy if I tried to stick with racing.

Jarrett managed jocks. The best I could do to stay close to the game was place bets on the ponies.

Me, I first heard the horses run on the radio. One thing I was always really good at was listening to Mister's radio. He'd be smoking those cigars Flo hated out back in that shack he had all to himself stuck sort of sideways onto the old six car garage and I'd be right outside one of the windows, the one he could never get all the way closed. Wasn't just me either. Lino Morelli and Paul Jarrett and a few others killed ourselves trying to keep quiet so we could listen to Jack Benny or Fred Allen or Burns and Allen—which wasn't easy, believe you me. More than once Paul or Lino or whoever had to stuff their shirts in their mouths to stifle the laughter. But when Mister switched the dial to the horse races everyone would drift off but me. Paul would listen for a race or three, but then he was gone too. There was something about the sound of the race caller, the noise from the crowd, the rhythm of pounding hooves. From the first, I was there, right there, heart beating along, and I wanted that world as much as, later, I wanted Bogie's world—before the war came along and made all those worlds even more precious knowing how easy they could all blow away. I must of heard every race Seabiscuit ever ran. It was Seabiscuit got me into this fix. I might have a lot more money stuffed in a sweet little bank account if I hadn't found racetracks. But probably not. I would of found some other way to get rid of it. Money just didn't seem to stick to me.

Mrs. Willingford was steaming when I got back to our table. Good thing she was too proud to do more than show it. But she did have a word to say about Paul.

"Joker likes that guy, but I never let him hire his jockeys."

"Why not?"

She started to open her mouth, started to say something. Then she closed it, turning her lips to thin strips of red rubber. At the same moment, I think we both knew she'd made a mistake. She couldn't tell me why not. So I knew why. The look on her face gave the whole game away. Because Paul may or may not have spent a little time in those cabins by the lake, but he'd never spent any with her. And from the look on mine, she knew I knew. She also knew she wouldn't be spending any with me. It must of shown in my eyes. Or the way my ears flapped. Or the way I couldn't finish the sidecar she'd ordered and paid for. Between her highhanded assumption I was not much more than a stable hand and my little chat with Paul, Mrs. Willingford's spell had faded dead away. Well, not completely, I admit that, but completely enough. It can happen that way and I was glad it did. The way she didn't look at the cabins, the way I felt I'd better get back to her table—or else, the laugh in Paul's voice when he implied I might have some trouble escaping Mrs. Willingford, all that and more told me I was just about to be somebody's pet poodle. One who could wind up in a pound.

Not Sam Russo, Staten Island's finest PI, not by a long shot. I gently pushed my barely touched drink over to her side of the table. "You probably need this more than me."

Mrs. Willingford stood up so fast the table thought about

going over. I grabbed both glasses to keep them smashing to the floor.

"I was mistaken. Good luck finding your own way back to town."

And she was out the door, had her zippy little roadster all revved up, and was gone in a fishtail of dust.

I looked at Paul and he looked at me and I had the best laugh I'd had in years.

It was about the last real honest laugh I'd have in Saratoga Springs. But I didn't know that at the time.

"Close call, pal," said Paul. "You'll have to come with me. 'Bout time I got back to work."

As we were walking out the door of the witch's house—what with this and that and the other, for me, Hansel and Gretel would always live in an oven at *Haven's Inn*—Paul called back over his shoulder. "Put it on my tab, right, Ray?"

It could of been my imagination, but Ray's response of "OK" didn't sound too excited. Like most barkeeps, he'd probably heard it too often from too many people. I wasn't surprised he was hearing it from Paul Jarrett. Paul was forever borrowing what little we had when we were kids. Sometimes we even got it back. With interest. Paul was the only kid I ever knew could calculate a rate of interest. Me and Lino were sure he'd go into banking.

Like Dillinger did.

15

After all the reading I'd done in my pink room in its pink hotel, I should of known to play my cards close to my chest. Marlowe did, Poirot did, Spade did. But this was Paul Jarrett, a kid I'd known since I could remember knowing anyone, and I needed someone to talk to. So all the way back to town, I talked. Or listened. The listening turned out pretty well. For one thing I learned why the track would hire a wet sock like the kewpie doll ex-cop for security. From Paul, I learned the genius' name was Carroll Goose. I wish I was kidding, but I'm not.

Paul, easy with his hands and feet, drove with a lot more care than Mrs. Willingford, and while he drove he gave me the low down. "Word's out, some of the types hang out at the tracks don't want good security. They have about two dozen scams in play at any given time on which good security could put the dampers. So they go looking for two-bit half wits to hire. Like Goose."

I had a moment's horror wondering if I was one of those two-bit half wits. But I shoved that into some part of my brain I seldom visited—and held it there, waiting for it to shut up.

Until getting hired by a track, all I knew about track management was what everyone else thought they knew about track management. They were men (a few rich widows and wives thrown in to make it interesting) who had a lot of money (don't ask how they got it; the answers you'd hear would be about as straight as a shell game on the Atlantic City boardwalk), and who liked to invest that money in pedigree horseflesh. For longer than the U.S. was the U.S., they formed jockey clubs (which your usual jockey never saw the inside of) and built race tracks where highbred horses competed in races of various sorts for various trophies and various purses (real purses, made of silk and hung on a line across the track for the winner to snatch).

In the beginning most of the jocks were rich guys like our first president. Old George, sitting bolt upright in the English style, competed up hill and down dale against other rich guys like himself. And then they all figured less weight was better and stuck their smallest black slaves on the back of their horses. Slaves began the style of riding crouched over and high on a horse's withers, and maybe they'd get a cut of their winnings and maybe they wouldn't. Some of 'em got so famous they were still names today: Isaac Murphy and Jimmy Winkfield and Willie Simms. But then the white kids noticed how good some of the black kids had it, so horned in on the action until every single black was cut out of the game. That was years ago.

What I really knew about was you might have a ticket on the one horse that came in first. Or the one that placed, which meant came in second. Or more often—a *lot* more often—you had a ticket that got tossed over your shoulder as you headed to the window for another hopeless bet. Come to think, I knew a great deal more than that about the sport. I knew about the trainers and the horses and the jocks and the races.

If I learned about the racetrack itself, I'd have the game covered.

Which is why I asked the question I now asked. "Some of the types? How can 'types' hire security?"

Paul laughed. "By some of the types, I included some of the types in the management category."

I'd been through one hell of a war. The scams that went on had once surprised and shocked me. You'd think I'd be beyond that kind of reaction. "You're telling me even management cheats their patrons?"

"I'm telling you even the owners of a track get involved. Not all, not all by any means, but a few. I'm telling you that Saratoga ain't immune. Although it's cleaner than most."

"So Goose got chosen because he's dumb?"

"Hell no! You have to be more than dumb to work security for these guys. You have to be greedy as well. And before you get the wrong idea, just like all the owners ain't in it, all management ain't in it either. And not every guy working as security is in their pocket. Like most things, it gets tricky to know who's what and how's that."

I sat in my seat for awhile, looking out at the trees and the little houses I'd never see the insides of and the farms where I'd never feed a chicken or milk a goat and just generally felt glum. "Great," I finally said.

"Great?"

"So who hired me? The good guys or the bad guys?"

"Beats me. A good guy can be a bad guy on any given day, and a bad guy can turn good on you when you least expect it."

"Thanks."

"You're welcome. And now let me ask you one."

"Shoot."

"What are you doing up here? I know it's not about the little scams always going on."

"Dead jocks."

"You're kidding. Me and everybody I know knows they're accidents."

"Everybody?"

Paul turned to give me one of his Clark Gable grins as we cruised into town and were passing all these swell American houses with their swell American front yards as we steered for Case Street. "Well, some of the jockeys aren't so sure, but you can't blame a jock for a little worry. Not when it's them doing the dying. But I tell my guys, and any of the others'll listen, bad luck always comes in threes."

"You believe that?"

"Of course not. But I do think three poor kids got into three stupid scrapes and I wish it hadn't happened to a single one of 'em, but there you go, these things happen."

I nodded. He could be right. It's certainly what the track officials wanted to hear. And I was pretty sure that's what I'd be telling them. But still. Three? Plus, there was something about the way Paul pronounced the word "scrapes" that made me wonder if he was also wondering, or if he was doing what everyone else was doing: humming along to Cole Porter's *It*

Was Just One of Those Things.

"Any one of them yours?"

He turned away when I asked him this. So I wouldn't see the pain in his eyes? So I wouldn't see the relief?

"God willing, no. And God willing not one of mine'll ever go down on the track either."

Amen to that one.

Paul dropped me off at my pink hotel and drove off like a mother with kids in the car. Jarrett had turned into a careful man. At least while driving.

He was headed for the racetrack. Guys like Paul Jarrett lived at whatever track they were working.

We were still seeing each other at eight, some place he knew where all the heavy handicappers ate. But just for a bite. No time to waste. I had to get some results here. So far, all I'd learned was that I had an old school tie at the Saratoga meet, that like at any track there were scams galore, that Mrs. Willingford could be had (although no longer by me; I couldn't say it broke my heart), and that the cop who'd stood over Pamela Teager was called Carroll Goose.

It didn't seem like much. And it wasn't.

There was a message waiting for me at the desk. It had its own little light brown envelope and the envelope was sealed. Nice touch. The kid at the desk didn't get to read it. If I were the kid at the desk, that would of ruined my day. Reading other people's mail had to be about the only perk he got. There couldn't be much else going on at the Pascal House. Pink houses, pink hotels, pink petunias didn't attract that kind of action.

All it said on the envelope was "Russo." It was written in pencil.

16

I threw my hat on the bed and loosened my tie. The tie was a sort of muddy greeny brown with little white flecks scattered over it—like lint. A present from a woman I once knew. Looking down at it, I wasn't sure she'd liked me all that much. I opened a window to get some air—catching a glimpse of the track through a mass of tiny climbing roses, tiny pink roses—took off my shoes, shook out a cigarette, threw myself in an easy chair, lit up and smoked. I looked at my envelope. Cheap. Thin. Common. You could buy hundreds of 'em for a quarter at your local five & dime. Too small for a letter or a bill, too big for those envelopes that come tucked away in a bunch of flowers. More than anything, it reminded me of a pay packet from one of those dying places that paid their employees in cash.

I didn't know why I wasn't just tearing it open. How often did I get notes in sealed envelopes. So far? Never. Maybe that's why I sat in a wingback chair upholstered in what looked like rosy cabbages in a pink room in a pink hotel, fouling up the hot summer air with cigarette smoke, and turning the thing round and round in my hands.

Then, with one quick move, I had it open and a small piece of torn newspaper fell in my lap. I didn't have to pick it up to read what it said—also in pencil.

33 Beekman Street. Room 7. Soon as you get this. It's worth your while.

I turned the bit of newspaper over. On the back I was offered an ice cold beer at the Tin 'N' Lint. Nothing else in pencil.

Worth my while? I wondered what that meant, but not for long. Anything was worth my while at the moment since as far as I could see, which was about as far as my feet, nothing had been so far. As for the address on Beekman Street, it

wasn't too far from the Gideon Putnam Burying Ground
where, a long time ago, everyone who was no one got
permanently planted. Among the nobodies was one certain
somebody; the actual Gideon Putnam who founded Saratoga
Springs as well as the Grand Union Hotel. He'd managed
to become the first resident of his new graveyard by taking
an accidental header off a scaffold in the middle of founding
some other first thing in Saratoga Springs. That was back
in 1812. Since then, pretty much no one had cared for the
place which made it the perfect setting for a Boris Karloff
movie. Graves were overgrown, gravestones overturned,
sections of the surrounding wall either crumbled away or
missing. As an area, everything west of Broadway was in the
same fix. 33 Beekman Street was some address—if a guy
needed a rat hole to hide in.

I learned all this at the library. I really was a curious
guy.

Meanwhile, I couldn't wait to have my time not wasted.

Hat back on, ugly tie straightened, I was out the door
half an hour after I walked in.

33 Beekman Street was everything I expected it to be.
Even in nice towns, rich towns, special towns like Saratoga
Springs where some of the most important, if not the
smartest or most honest, people hang their hats, there's
always an area like the area Beekman ran through. There
had to be someplace for the hired help to live, for the drunks
and the deadbeats and the family man with too much family
and too little job. The building I walked towards fit the bill
perfectly.

I rang the buzzer next to a crudely drawn 7 and was
buzzed in as fast as everything else was happening.

The guy behind the barely opened door was small.
Really small. Jockey small. The room behind the small guy
had just enough furniture to suit someone who had nothing
to do and thick enough curtains to make sure no one saw
him not doing it.

I got my sleeve grabbed and was in the room before I could
get my gun out. But since my gun was still in my suitcase
back at my pretty pink palace, it didn't much matter.

"You wanna drink?" said the little man.

Before I could answer, he was drinking straight from the bottle, a half full pint—or half empty if you're one of those kind of people. Whichever, I passed on his offer.

"Sit down. Sit down. I can't sit down. Can't sit still for that long. Be nice to see someone else doin' it. What was I saying?"

"Sit down."

"Nah. Before that."

"I wasn't here before that."

"You weren't?" He gave his bottle a look like it was up to no good, then took another pull.

I sat on the only chair in the room, one never made to actually sit on. Unless it was designed for slow torture. That lasted maybe ten seconds and I was up and walking around with him.

"Listen, shamus." And with that crack he was pointing one of his tiny fingers at me. I had no idea why. I just let him do it. "Don't ask how I know you're a snoop, everyone knows you're a snoop for the track bigwigs. And everyone knows they want you to smooth things over and then beat it back to the hole you crawled out of."

I flicked something off my sleeve. I thought it was a bug. I hoped it was a bug. "No need to get nasty, chum. I am, after all, an invited guest in your lovely home."

One of his eyes focused. "Sorry. I'm jumpy is all. Can you imagine? I got a mount in the third and the fifth today."

All I could imagine, watching him put away the hard stuff, is what us poor saps at the betting windows never get to know.

"Did I tell you my name?"

"If so, I missed it."

"I'm Mash Mooney."

"Mooney! I've bet on you. More than once."

"You have?" Mash said that like he'd just won the Belmont Stakes. "Then I got no call to be doing you down. But still I gotta know. You in their pocket or you really lookin'?"

"I don't know where *they* think I am, but I'm really looking."

"How do I believe you?"

"No idea. You do or you don't. You wrote the note."

"Right. The note." He pointed at me with his pint of rye or whatever it was. Maybe a spoonful of it landed on the worn carpet between us. "I wrote you so's you'd come here and I could tell you what I know."

"What do you know?"

"Manny Walker din't drown."

"How's that?"

"He din't drown. He didn't even go swimmin'. I mean he usually went swimmin', but that morning he din't."

Right there, I could of asked him all kinds of questions but it seemed best to let him talk. Especially since he was talking more to his bottle than to me and to some guys bottles make the best listeners.

"Him and me, we was out all night at the Tin 'N' Lint, even with the races comin' up, and when we got back, it was too late for that swimmin' he liked to do. So he din't do it. Instead, we just thought we'd get some shuteye at our bunks at the track and he could swim twice as long the next day. Only Manny didn't get a next day, did he?"

"If you have a bunk at the track, why are you here?"

"Hiding. Whatchoo think? I don't wanna wind up like Manny."

"Right. How do you know Manny didn't get up anyway after you were asleep and go off by himself?"

"'Cause he was gone as soon as he hit the mattress, and I mean gone, like nuthin' could of woke him. Me, it couldn't have taken much longer. But it's a twenty minute drive out to the lake if you go the way he'd always go. Which, by the way, you have to go because that's where the county road goes. When I woke up, his car was still outside our shed. He din't borrow nobody else's. I asked. So it's like this. We bunk down, plastered as a coupla walls, at 4:29 a.m. Manny's asleep at 4:30 a.m. I know. I got this watch— "

He showed me his watch. Pretty nice watch.

"Plus, I saw him and it wasn't some fake. Why should he fake? Who could fake that loud? Yet that old man in the rowboat found him face down without a snorkel at 4:45 a.m.

That's gotta mean he gets up immediately he's asleep, not to mention me being asleep a foot away and I don't notice a thing, gets his trunks on, doesn't take a towel, they didn't find no towel, doesn't drive to the lake which he can't make in that kind of time without his car, and which is hard enough to do even in something like some of these rich dames drive, and somehow winds up dead all in less than 15 minutes. You tell me how that could happen?"

17

I stood there in Mash's crummy room looking down at Mash who was looking up at me. Truth was, he'd just described a magic trick. Even if it was an accident, how the hell did Manny get found dead in a lake before he had time to get to it?

This was looking like a case for Sherlock Holmes, or at least someone with more brains than I had.

Inside and out, Saratoga Springs was beginning to get hot and the heat was creating a lot of humidity. The town was water water everywhere: lakes, springs, rivers, and all that water was mixing with the air. Time to stop wearing a hat and tie. Time for a sport shirt and loafers. Or maybe a pair of swim trunks. Only I didn't bring any.

So I walked around the room with Mash and I sweated for a while thinking about how Manny Walker could be sound asleep in bed at the Saratoga race track one minute and then floating in pond weed fifteen minutes later. For the life of me, I couldn't work it out.

Mash had finished the pint of rye. I could tell if he had another bottle, he'd be working on that one. But he didn't, so he played with the empty he had. Rubbing it like Aladdin's lantern, sticking his finger in it, then pulling it out. That much booze in his system, I would of thought he'd be cockeyed, but he seemed sober as a nightclub bouncer. Even so, the kid was beginning to get on my nerves.

"You expect to ride full of hootch?"

"No one kills me, I can ride any old way."

Before they fully formed, I banished the voices I suddenly heard in my head. *We'll get the little bastards. No one can kill me. No one can kill my horse.* Until we ourselves killed our horses for food, horses that had gallantly carried us to victory against the first Japanese attempt against Bataan. For about a second, I came close to lapping up Mash's spilled hootch. I had a lot of bad memories—the Bataan Death March for instance—but coming *this* close to making that march myself took the prize for bad memories. "That's good to hear. Now how about Babe Duffy? You think he really choked to death on his lunch? Or McBartle. He drives into a tree completely sober and never even tries to brake?"

Mash hadn't stopped pacing for a minute. When he answered, he was behind the straight backed chair I started out suffering on. "I don't know. I don't know. All I know is all three of 'em had mounts in the Travers and now they don't. And I didn't have a mount in the Travers and now I do. The trainer of Hornet's Nest asked my agent for me. He had to ask George—"

"George Labold." I wasn't asking. I was just thinking out loud.

"Yeah, him. So I get the ride 'cause the leading jocks are already booked—or dead. And as for McBartle's Court'n Spark, George had to actually dig up a jockey who'd gone and retired. Jimmy Sparkle, a great rider."

"Damn. I remember Sparkle. He won practically everything in his time."

"You said it. And he can still win."

"Labold's McBartle's agent too?"

"Uhuh. But Manny was up on Fleeting Fancy and Fleeting Fancy is as good as they come. She can beat the colts most anytime. Like that big filly, Gallorette, the one Kirkland just rode even though they had her weighted down like they think she's Beldame or somethin'. But as for Fleeting Fancy, her people ain't found their rider yet. You can bet every kid like me from here to California is begging for that ride."

I thought of the boy with the moon in his eyes I saw standing looking at Fancy when I was doing the exact same thing. What was his name? Toby something or other. No longer a bug boy, but a legit jock.

"Anyway, you'd think all this was a great break for me. You know, Babe Duffy losing the mount I now got, but somehow it makes me sick in the guts. It don't smell right and I couldn't say why. Which is why I'm here. I ain't hanging around the track unless I got to ride, and I'm gone as soon as I win or lose."

Mash threw himself on the lumpy bed which made one hell of a lot of creaking when he did it, while I did some thinking. He was right. Something not only didn't smell right, it stank. And if Manny wasn't an accident, then the odds were pretty good that the other two weren't accidents either.

But if they weren't accidents, then what were they?

Murder? Why murder three young promising jockeys?

I needed something really simple, something any cop or PI needed, and that was called a motive. I didn't have a motive. Although I did have a glimmer of an idea how Manny could of drowned in a lake that took fifteen minutes to get to by car.

I looked around. What a location. What a room. What a chair. I didn't envy Mash Mooney hiding out in it. But I understood it.

I finally asked the obvious question. "You've told the police all this?"

In return I received a look you'd see on a guy paying good money for a freak show and getting a faceful of cats with six toes. "Are you nuts? You think the cops want to hear what I got to say? This town don't believe in murder. Besides, I *did* say it. Or at least I started to. Some badge came by later on the day Manny died and asked a question or two. I tried to answer, but right out of the gate I could tell he wasn't listenin', so I shut up."

That made sense. I'd seen Lino do that a few times. Once he thought he had a case solved, it was solved. And once he thought there was no case, it disappeared. Another reason I wanted to be a PI and not a cop. Also why I hadn't bothered any of Saratoga's finest. I already knew this kind of thing went on. If whoever was paying for my time wanted three murders to be three accidents, then it only followed the police wanted the same thing.

I was really on my own here. Very comforting. Very Bogie.

"Listen kid. Do what you have to do. You know where I

am if you need me. But right now I have to check something out."

"You're saying you believe me?"

"I'm saying I wish I didn't."

"Damn damn and double damn." With that, he turned on his side and curled up with his empty bottle like a little kid afraid of the dark.

I left him there like that. I was a private investigator, not a babysitter.

18

From Beekman, I caught a cab to the track. Nothing's too far from anything else in the Spa, not if you're only there for the racing, so there aren't that many cabs needed, but I required all the time I could get and, what do you know, cruising Washington Street was a rare and empty cab—so I grabbed it.

I'd heard from someone who'd heard it from someone that Carl Hessing was up here running horses in a couple of the claiming races. Hessing owed me a favor. It wasn't a big favor, but calling in any size marker on Hessing wasn't easy. Sam Russo, Staten Island's greatest—and only Private Eye—needed to try.

Hessing was the only guy I knew in Saratoga who had what I needed to work out how Manny Walker could get from a bed where he'd passed out stinking drunk, and into an off-track lake faster than Jesse Owens in the 100 meter dash. And how he wouldn't wake the fuck up from the shock of it and not swim the easy three feet back to shore.

All I needed was two things. The first was a good map of Saratoga Springs. That part was easy. My little hotel gave 'em out for free. The second part wasn't so easy. I had to get my hands on one of Carl's claiming horses. It didn't have to be a world beater—which was good since Carl didn't have any world beaters. But it did have to be agile and fearless and I had to convince Carl he'd get it back in the same shape it started out in. If not, he had to trust I'd somehow replace it with a horse of equal quality. Knowing Carl Hessing, "equal" meant he'd expect me to show up with Exterminator.

All Carl cared about were *his* horses. Nothing sentimental about it. Carl was a mercenary. If a nag was never in the money, he sold said nag to a slaughter house. I never got round to hating people. Hate took too much energy. But I

disliked a lot of 'em. I disliked Carl Hessing like I disliked
the Zawadzkis.

Standing there, looking at the condition of his animals,
I got to disliking him more than the Zawadzkis. Flo and
Mister were nuts. Carl was a snake.

Too bad. I needed him.

It took half an hour to persuade him. I told him how
good I'd once been as his exercise rider. And I had been.
Exercising a horse took skill. Horses would lean on the
bit. Or they'd buck. Or they'd lug in or lug out, tossing
their heads. Sometimes they'd jump a rail or run through an
opening not big enough for them, much less for me. Carl
wasn't listening. So I threw in the charge on horseback
against the Japanese at Bataan. Carl liked the war since he
hadn't seen it.

I ended up giving him ten bucks to rent what had to be
War Admiral's worst son, a dark bay gelding called Skysail.

War Admiral was not only the son of Man o' War, he'd
won the 1937 Kentucky Derby, the 1937 Preakness, the
1937 Belmont Stakes, the 1938 Whitney Handicap, and the
1938 Jockey Club Gold Cup. He lost his match race with
Seabiscuit, but you can't win 'em all. Not even Man o' War
won 'em all. The Admiral's son, Skysail, started 12 times
with a record of no wins, one third, and the rest out of the
money. War Admiral's get was a 5 year old gelding and rode
like a kid's soapbox cart. No one called him Skysail—a name
I might of bet on back when my idea of handicapping was a
"lucky" number and a name that caught my eye. I was nine.

Carl called him Abandon Ship, or Shippy for short.
Shippy and I didn't start off well. Why, I couldn't say. Hell,
I liked horses. Shippy tried bucking me off, then he tried
scraping me off against the side of a barn, then knocking me
off under a low hanging branch. No dice. I was still there.
So he gave up, settled down, and agreed to join me on this
idea I had, one I got listening to Mash Mooney.

When he rode during the Saratoga season—only twice;
the kid was still so young—Manny Walker drove out the
back gate of the track, along a short country road, before
taking a right onto a decent dirt road through dense woods

that gradually got less and less drivable, until he had to park and walk a few hundred feet to the lake of his choice. There were three of 'em in the woods southeast of the racecourse. No matter how fast he drove and no matter if the road was paved right up to the water's edge, he couldn't of got there in time. Forget getting dead. He had no time for dying at all. But, if someone had gone behind the barns, opened a little used side gate in the track's main fence, and rode through on a horse, it could of been done easily—with time to spare.

Even Shippy made the distance without half trying. We found out by doing it. If we'd wanted to go, there were narrow deer trails through the trees that could of taken us to town, to any one of the three lakes, even to the neighboring state of Vermont. All we wanted to do was canter to the right lake, mess around for a few minutes, and canter back. No one, unless they were also on the deer trail, would of seen us in full daylight, much less in the dark. It hadn't been totally dark. I'd checked. That night, the moon had been a waning gibbous. I had to look that up. It meant the moon was still large but getting smaller. It meant there was light enough to see in the woods if a guy was careful. And a horse can see a lot better than a man can.

It took us five minutes to get to the lake. It would of taken another three or four minutes for whoever had Manny slung over his saddle to get the kid into his swim trunks so he could toss him in the drink. Manny was drunk. He'd passed out in bed. I doubt he woke up on the ride. If the shock of cold water brought him round, he'd still be drunk, disoriented and scared. He could be pushed back under until it was all over.

It didn't matter too much how long it took his killer to get back to the track because however long it was, he was gone from the lake five minutes at least before Herb Bedwell, the old duffer out predawn rowboat fishing, paddled up. If it was me, I'd know it was a good idea to get whatever horse I used back before all the other horses and their stable-mates started to wake up—which could start as early as 5 a.m. If a horse woke up earlier, along with its stable boy or its donkey or its chicken or its goat or whatever kept it company, I'd say

I'd had the horse out of his stall for an early morning walk.

That didn't happen because if it did, you'd think someone would of said so.

Shippy and me, we learned this much: whoever was doing what they were doing was one lucky killer. You could be smart as Capablanca the chess player (though why playing chess was considered smart beats me; even I can play chess and I play it well—all it takes is the ability to think ahead and stay awake), but to kill three people, hell, to kill even one person, takes a thick dusting of luck.

What we didn't find were tracks. But no tracks didn't bother me too much. It was summer. The ground was hard. If anything, the hooves of the other horse would of done only what Shippy's hooves had done: kick up the leaves. Any killer worth his salt had plenty of time and privacy to walk along the same path and brush everything back into place. As for there being no horse tracks by the edge of the lake, the killer probably stopped before he got there, then carried Manny, no bigger than a 15 year old kid and weighing no more than a hundred and fifteen pounds, tops, out onto the small dock at the edge of the water. No need to get his (or her) feet wet, no need to disturb the muck on the bottom of the lake.

I still had no idea *why* he was killed, but I was sure now that Manny didn't just drown. Manny Walker *was* drowned. And if he was drowned, then the next thing I needed to know was what really happened to McBartle and Duffy. But this time, I had to go about it with a lot more care, because this time, I wasn't looking for proof of an accident. This time I'd be going against what everyone was expecting or hoping or counting on.

Someone, probably connected with the track and probably Marshall Hutsell, was probably watching every move I made, pleased I hadn't done anything to bother anyone.

Now I had.

I was easy to find. I lived in a pink hotel.

Walking away from the low end barns, I collided with George Labold. I knew what I was doing, I was thinking hard about how Walker got his, but I didn't get what Labold was doing. Jockey's agents stuck around the trainers and the owners, working to get their clients up on the best mounts they could wrangle.

Labold didn't bother with claimers. Not enough money in it.

"Lost, George?"

I'd confused him.

"No. I was… I was just… "

"Following me around?"

That was meant as a joke. But George didn't look like he thought it was funny.

"Following you? What the hell would I follow you for?"

A second later, he was off for the nearest shed row, sprinting on legs as long as Fleeting Fancy's.

I could of given that more thought. But all I was thinking about was three dead jockeys, a police department already calling them accidents, me being maybe no more than another Carroll Goose, a scared jock in a crummy room in a crummy part of town, and a woman called Mrs. Willingford.

Why the hell was I thinking of Mrs. Willingford?

19

Working with Lino Morelli, I'd learned some basic facts about choosing the life of a PI.

One: you were on your own. Unlike Lino with his police force and his politicians, there was no one to back your plays. There were no central files you could rifle through. No way to check fingerprints. No way to look at photos. Or to trace phone calls.

Two: any ideas you had were yours and yours alone. If you didn't have any ideas, you couldn't hide behind the next cop saying, I agree with him.

Three: whatever you did could get you laughed at or it could get you killed. Ditto for what you didn't do. You getting killed wouldn't matter much to the cops. They wouldn't do anything about it. To a cop, a PI was someone who got in the way or got themselves dead.

Four: cops had authority. PIs didn't. No authority meant you had to be a smooth mover and a fast talker.

I could've gone on like this, but I needed to be getting on with stuff like: what the hell should I do next? If the killer owned a horse or trained a horse or did pretty much anything with a horse, I wasn't going to find him (or her) by asking if anyone'd done what I'd done. In other words, did anyone borrow a horse on the morning in question? Besides, at a track, the horse might not need borrowing—a simple taking of your own horse would do. Trouble was, racehorses were not ponies. They weren't docile. They weren't used to being ridden anywhere but on a racetrack. You couldn't depend on any one of them to trot along a path in the dark carrying weight they'd never been trained to carry, or even tolerate. OK, so it wasn't a Thoroughbred. It wouldn't be a Thoroughbred. But it could of been a stable pony or a companion to a high strung racehorse.

I decided asking around was a poor idea.

Best to move on to poking around in the death of one of the other jockeys.

Babe Duffy choked to death on a ham sandwich. He'd been alone except for his loyal dog. Dogs don't talk. No one was hiding out writing me penciled notes from cheap rooming houses about what he knew about Duffy. I'd leave Duffy and his dog for last.

That left Matthew Mark McBartle. Another kid who got up in the middle of the night, not a swimmer but a driver.

McBartle didn't bunk at the track. He was much too successful for that. Or much too profligate. Or maybe just vain. He'd taken a room at the most expensive joint in town, the Grand Union Hotel. That was the one with the parking lot the size of Madison Square. Or the park near my place over on Staten Island.

I wondered which room was his. I wondered where he kept his car. I wondered how he looked to the night clerk when he crossed the lobby at 3:15 in the morning. Had he said anything? Did he seem unusual? I'd heard he was alone. Was he really?

Only way to find out was to ask. Even if asking could get me more attention than I was sure I'd already attracted.

Half way across the Grand Union's parking lot, the same one I'd first crossed escaping the company of Carroll Goose, moving through cars I'd only seen in advertisements, I got a big surprise. Out of nowhere, just strolling along, I was jumped. Never suspected it for a second; didn't even see 'em coming. Two guys, one big and one small, both with that look of an inner city boxing ring about 'em: bent noses, cauliflower ears, distorted hands, the sneer that came with a complete lack of brains. I didn't know what Bogie would of done, but what I did was protect myself the best I could. I had a gun, but that was back at my pink hotel.

I was never one for fighting. Or shooting people. I usually got out of any fix I was in by running or riding—or talking—as fast as I could.

Not this time. This time I barely got out a yelp before I was lying curled up on the ground. There was blood but no missing teeth. That was good. Dentists didn't come cheap. I could barely see, barely move, barely hear. I'd been beaten up before, but that was just kid stuff back at the old school. This was bad. It hurt. It scared me. I was ashamed. My ears were roaring but I caught what the smaller one said, aiming a kick at my kidneys. "Boss says you come near his wife again and you'll get more'n this. S'long, sucker."

Quiet settled over me like dirt over a coffin.

All alone with a terrific view of a brand new Goodyear tire, every bit of me hurting, a mouth full of blood—I used the time to ponder. Pondering suited a face full of parking lot cement. Who else was I supposed to think "the boss" was if it wasn't Joker Willingford? I didn't buy it. A man as old and as rich as Joker was, an old man married to a woman like Mrs. Lois Willingford, knew what he had. He had a showpiece. He wouldn't care what she got up to as long as it didn't cost him too much and as long as it didn't embarrass him more than just getting old all by itself was embarrassing. Maybe I'd just gotten beaten up for not taking a tour of a cabin by a lake with Mrs. Willingford. Maybe that's how she worked. Could be she didn't like men, period. That made me ponder what she might think of boys who snubbed her, or young kids, or up and coming jockeys.

Or—the whole Willingford involvement was a ruse to divert me from the real killer.

Flat out on asphalt, I stared at the tire some more. Jesus, look at those whitewalls. Nifty. But nah. What killer would hire two goons to kick the crap out of me so one could make a crack about "the boss"?

I said I played chess, a tedious game of anticipating an opponent's move as far in advance as possible. This would be one hell of a stupid move; one that would make the killer vulnerable to two professional morons.

That left only three other possibilities. The goons had made a mistake; they beat up the wrong mark. Or, the guys running rackets at the track would like me to go home now. Or, the guys who'd hired me to prove Saratoga Springs was the site of three accidents, not three murders, weren't pleased at how my work was going. In their own way, they were telling me to stop working. So—they spent more money on goons? Why not just fire me?

Which rich goofball would be that crude and that stupid? Easy. Marshall Hutsell, rich goofball. Hutsell hired the muscle.

No need to work out how Hustsell knew what I was up to. A vision of George Labold idled into my mind. If George was their snoop hired to snoop on their hired snoop, it made me sad. To see a good agent fall so far.

If it was George.

I couldn't lie here admiring my tire forever. I had to drag myself up, brush myself down, wince with pain—a kidney punch really hurt, deep down hurt—spit blood until I was sure when I smiled I wouldn't frighten the horses.

I did think I'd smile again. But I didn't know when.

The contents of the bar of the Grand Union Hotel called to me.

I had a look at my shoes, my pants, my jacket. If I could get through one of its grand doors without making a scene, I was sure to find a Gentleman's toilet and could get all gorgeous again.

20

The gents at the Grand Union wasn't kidding. It was grand. A bunch of big mirrors in big frames, fancy washbasins and gold fixtures—even a row of marbled urinals. It had Louis the whatever chairs scattered about and real palms in real pots which someone really watered. It had brass spittoons and free cigarettes in a big black lacquer box and free cigars in a bigger red lacquer box. There were gold dragons on the boxes and a huge golden horse made of what looked like real gold racing across one maroon colored wall. It had an aging black man with his own lacquered cubicle who was there just to shine your shoes if they needed it. Mine needed it.

The gentleman's attendant's name was Thomas Clay Jefferson. He lived up to every inch of it. If there was a single soul cluttering up a single inch of the Grand Union who could truly be said to look like a gentleman, that soul was Thomas Clay Jefferson. He had a lot of grey in his short kinky hair and his hands would of looked good on Nat King Cole. I didn't know about the voice. Not many, if any, could touch Cole's voice. He wasn't pretty. His left eye was what they called a lazy eye—sometimes it looked where the right eye was looking and sometimes it didn't—but just the same, looking at him made me feel good. I told him to call me Sam. He said he'd call me sir but I could call him Clay. I told him I was a PI. I told him I was looking into the deaths of Saratoga's three jockeys. And then, while he made me look better than I have ever looked, I found myself telling him my entire life story right up to the moment I walked into his gentleman's lounge.

I never found a better listener. If I could of voted for him for President of these United States, I would of.

That'll be the day.

"They didn't touch your face much, sir," he said, gently

removing tar from my right hand.

"Not much you can do to a face like mine, Clay. So why the blood in my mouth?"

"You have a fine face. Reminds me of Robert Mitchum. Interior bleeding, sir. You might want to see a doctor."

"And then again, I might not. Never had a good feeling about doctors."

His right eye smiling directly into mine, his left doing whatever it wanted to, Clay grinned.

I said, "Not Humphrey Bogart? And before you can say it, I know Bogie's not a doctor."

I almost got a laugh.

"No, sorry, sir. Definitely Robert Mitchum."

I was going to have to go see a Robert Mitchum film. After this job, I could probably afford the two bits for a movie ticket. If I lived through it. The job, not the movie.

There are some ways in which it pays to be beaten up. Whoever the thugs worked for, they were the cause of my introduction to Thomas Clay Jefferson. That alone was worth it. Clay not only listened, he talked. Whenever the classy gents was emptied out of those who might loosely be considered gents, he told me what I would never hear anywhere else. For one thing, the coroner was the brother of his wife's second best friend. This added up to a lot of people in Saratoga Springs, not rich or influential, not even connected to the horse racing industry, who knew Babe Duffy did not choke to death on his ham sandwich, not without help. The coroner'd told his sister—Clay's wife's second best friend—who'd told a bunch of people, including Clay's wife, that he had his doubts about Babe choking. Babe Duffy could of done no more than choke, true, but he could also of had more than half a sandwich shoved down his throat and held there until he suffocated. It was possible. There were marks on his jaw bearing this out. The biggest thing Clay told me the coroner said: "You know what the mayor said to me privately? He said if you'd just write down 'accidental death,' it would go a long way towards helping you keep your job."

The season paid the bills in Saratoga Springs. No one

wanted the season spoiled.

Clay was proud to report that the brother of his wife's friend did not take this lying down. Not as the coroner, but as a private citizen, he was saying to those he trusted (no fool, that guy): "If I ever get a chance to get up in court and answer under oath, me being the official coroner with my reputation on the line, I'd state clear as a bell that it *is* possible Babe Duffy stuffed an entire ham sandwich into his mouth and tried to swallow it whole. But I'll also ask: is this feasible? Who would do something like that? I'd say if it *was* suicide, it was the weirdest damn suicide I've ever heard of. I'd also say that if it was murder, it was also goddamn strange. I've never heard of death by sandwich of any kind. Choking on a wad of gum, now that's happened. Choking on most anything, that's happened too. But who would try and cram that much food in their mouth all at once? A person wouldn't die, his own bodily reflexes would hack the damn thing right back out. Same goes if it was an accident. Basically I'd say it's unprecedented. And on top of that, suicide or murder or accident, that dog that he had, the one that can't bark—a basangi? a besoobi?—didn't take it lightly. I was there. I saw it. All around the body near the mineral spring, his paw prints were everywhere. And some seemed to show the dog being shoved backwards. I'd tell the inquest those paw prints were cleaned up fast. Right in front of me. So what I'd swear to, on oath, is I only wrote 'death by accident' to keep my job. But if I could have, I would have written 'death by circumstances unknown.' And that's what I'd say if asked."

I said: "He said all that? In that order? Damn."

"Indeed, sir. As close as I can remember. I could of embellished some. I'm partial to embellishment. But yes sir, he said most of all that. And might I offer some advice?"

"You might."

"Don't go askin' questions of just anyone around this place. You come back here one o'clock in the mornin', maybe two o'clock, and you talk to a young negro fella named Alonzo. He runs elevator 9. You remember that number and that name?"

"I'll remember."

"And don't you be talkin' where anybody sees you."

"Gotcha."

"Alonzo set you straight. Meanwhile, you just have yourself a quick drink and then you get yourself out of here. This ain't the place a man everyone knows is lookin' out for them dead jocks should be seen."

I thanked Thomas Clay Jefferson. I handed him a large tip. He took half, handed the other half back. The first half he folded neatly and placed carefully under the cigars in the red lacquer box. "A thing's worth what a thing's worth. Dig up the truth, sir. Cain't have folks goin' about hurtin' other folks like that."

I said I'd be back. I told him I'd let him know what I knew. He smiled at me, a smile as warming as a winning ticket.

"You come see me whenever you please. I about live here. But there's one thing I won't have."

I gave myself one last lingering look in a full length mirror—Mitchum? I didn't have a cleft in my chin, did I? I did, on the other hand, look half asleep, but that wasn't surprising since I'd just got the stuffing kicked out of me.

Absorbed in myself, I turned back to hear what Clay wouldn't have.

Both his eyes were staring directly into mine. "Don't let me see you lyin' on my wife's second best friend's brother's slab."

That made my goodbye smile fall off.

21

I should of known who'd be holding forth at the main bar of the Grand Union Hotel.

As soon as I'd eased myself onto a stool—Clay may have groomed me as well they once groomed Black Gold, but my kidney ached like hell—I looked over and there she was, Mrs. Too-willing-ford. We both glanced away at the same time. I don't know what or who she was looking at then, but I was staring at a nose the size of Mount Rushmore. I knew who owned it immediately. A famous nose like that, beloved at race tracks everywhere, belonged to the jockeys' agent who'd handled both Manny Walker and Babe Duffy. Hollie Hayes was drinking straight bourbon out of a coffee cup (those old Prohibition habits die hard) looking worse than I did, even in his usual unusual selection of clothes. From shoes to hat, the man dressed like Bugs Bunny when Bugs Bunny was dressing like Red Skelton. As for crying in his beer, who could blame him? More than half his income had just died "accidently."

Taking a quick look over my shoulder, I got an eyeful of who Mrs. Willingford was looking at. I had to hand it to him. Paul Jarrett was always a fast one. He'd changed his shirt. It was still Hawaiian, but this one was lime green with parrots on it.

Mrs. Willingford looked like she'd changed her mind about using his jockeys. And if not, they were negotiating something. Paul was doing his elbows on table, leaning in close, thing. Made me chuckle. After him warning me off. One of the things I always found myself thinking about went like this: I'd never stop being embarrassed by people.

I caught Paul's eyes and winked. Paul had skin as thick as a rhino's. He winked back.

I took Thomas Clay Jefferson's advice. I got myself out

of the grand Grand Union downing one drink and one drink only. I wasn't going to see Alonzo the elevator operator about McBartle until at least one in the a.m. I had a lot of day left ahead of me. What to do now?

What I wanted to do was catch a movie. There were two new Bogie movies playing in town: something called *Key Largo* with Bacall. I liked Bacall well enough (she was no Carole Lombard, but she had a nice set of—teeth), but Bogie wasn't playing a PI. And something without Bacall called *The Treasure of the Sierra Madre*. He wasn't a PI in that either.

No time for a movie. I needed to check up on Carroll Goose, see if what he was hired for hooked up with what I was hired for. If he was, I'd go to the movies, bet the races, file a report of death by accident, and go home.

I walked through the gates of the Saratoga race track right about the time the third was going off. Oddest feeling in the world to be at a track and not have the foggiest who was running in what and who was riding who. I'd been in this situation before, but even then I'd get a bet down. Early days. Innocent days. Big loss days.

Goose wasn't hard to find. He was where all the other security guards were: in an employee's lounge. I called it a lounge because that's what everyone was doing. Compared to Thomas Clay Jefferson's gentlemen's lounge at the Grand Union, it was a French open toilet. With most of the track "security" stuffed in it, I thought about how many Abba Zabba bars were being filched from the vending machines. As for all the other no-nos going on at the track, I imagined it was one hell of a free-for-all. Every flim flam invented by man was in full swing.

Drinking hootch out of a Dixie cup, Goose was lying back on a couch rejected by the Salvation Army.

"Hi ya, Russo!"

"Afternoon, Goose."

"Where d'ja get the fat lip?"

"*The Finish Line*. One-day-only-sale."

Goose thought about that long enough to get beaten to the laugh by half the other guys there.

A guy over by a wire-glass window with a mouth on him as wide as his face, said, "Who's your pal, Goose?" Once I saw him, I couldn't stop looking, and not because his badge said *Head of Security*, not just *Security*.

"This is my pal, Sam Russo. He's a PI out of Staten Island."

All smiles were off and all backs turned. Carroll Goose found this surprising. "Hey guys. That's rude. This here is my best pal."

Even though it cost me—kidney gave out a little scream only I could hear—I raised a hand. "Well, not— "

"Me an' him was on a case together. A *murder* case."

"Carroll? Will you step over here a moment, please?"

"Sure." He brought his hair, his moustache, his breath and his Dixie Cup. "What's up?"

"You heard who's riding Fleeting Fancy in the Travers?"

Goose rubbed his head which ruined his comb-over. "Now I did hear something about that. First it was supposed to be some jock out of California. Then I heard it might be this really young kid named, uh, named… "

"Toby Tyrrell?"

"Hey, yep, sure, that sounds about right."

"You happen to know who agents him?"

"Me? Why would I know that? I don't even know what it means."

"It means all jockeys have someone who helps them get mounts. You know, a horse to ride in a race? For that, the someone, called a jockeys' agent, takes a cut of the jockey's cut."

"Yeah? That's really, you know, interestin'. But hey, I just got here. Wha'd I say? Great job, right?"

"It suits you."

Goose grinned, a huge grin for such a small face. I noticed his teeth were as small as seed pearls and as white as White King Soap.

Ten minutes later, in the jockey's dressing room, I found Toby Tyrrell suiting up for the fifth. Egg yolk yellow silk shirt with a crimson cap. White silk breeches with the same shade of yellow stripe down the outside of the leg. A yellow

pompom on top of the crimson cap. I knew those colors.
They were the silks of a fair-to-middling operation with a
few good horses. Not great, but honest. Treated their horses
well. Tyrrell had the mount on the second favorite, a nicely
set up dappled gray filly called You Don't Know Me.

The kid was about as interested in me as I was interested
in sitting through a fashion show at Bergdorf. So I leaned
up against a wall, scratched a match on a pillar, and smoked.
I stared at him while I did this. It only took a minute or
so to unnerve him. People hate being stared at by people,
especially strange people. And I had a fat lip. I also apparently
resembled Robert Mitchum.

Finally the kid walked right up to me and spoke directly
into my belt buckle. "You ain't gonna like what happens you
keep staring at me."

I looked down at the top of his curly head of dark brown
hair and kept staring. Which forced him to look up. So then
we both stared at each other. He was a really good looking
kid. Sort of Tyrone Power without the girliness.

"What's going to happen if I keep staring at you?"

He thought about his answer long enough for me to
answer for him. "Thugs? Banned from the track? No more
allowance?"

I made him smile. That was good.

"You get the pickup mount on Fleeting Fancy?"

"Who's askin'?"

"Me."

"Yeah. I got the horse."

"You happy?"

"You kiddin?"

"How do you feel about how you got it?"

"Accidents happen. That my fault?"

"Three accidents?"

The kid jock looked at his feet. He looked at a locker.
He looked at a set of silks on a peg. He did not look at me.
"Ain't sayin' it ain't sorta spooky."

"Spooky enough to make *you* worry?"

"About what?"

"Your accident."

For that I got a sound like a goldfish blowing bubbles at the top of his bowl and a flap of the kid's hand—like he was warding off evil. When he finally spoke, it was more a whisper than a lowered voice. "Yeah. OK. Sure. I'm spooked."

"So you don't think they were accidents?"

"I don't know," he wailed in a quiet sort of way. There was a lot of despair in that little wail. "I just don't know."

That made two of us. But one of us was beginning to get a picture forming in his mind. Hazy. Still full of holes. But a picture nonetheless.

22

I hung about for a bit, smoked a few cigarettes, nursed a few beers watching Toby Tyrrell bring You Don't Know Me home by four lengths in a hand ride. A few feet away a coupla heavy betters talked about the kid's way with a horse, that they'd be watching out for him from now on, but the dappled gray filly wasn't bad either. Mostly they were working out who to bet on in the Travers Stakes. Could this new jock bring home Fleeting Fancy like he brought home You Don't Know Me? Was there a point in betting a filly against colts? And how about that Gallorette, taller than a lot of the males? And, oh boy, was she faster. In '45 she'd beaten Hoop Jr. who'd won the Kentucky Derby that year. Still going up against males, she took second in the Wood Memorial. She beat Stymie. She'd won the Carter Handicap as well as, a few days back, the Whitney. Hard to bet against her. They both licked the ends of their pencil stubs. But then, said one, there was Fleeting Fancy, another female up against males. Fleeting Fancy won less races than Gallorette but she won easier. The other said: she was also younger.

Hard call, said one. You bet, said the other.

Listening to all that, I got sleepier and sleepier. It'd already been some day. I'd fed Carroll Goose a nourishing breakfast of booze, read a lot of newspapers at the office of *The Saratogian*, got taken for a ride by a woman who thought I could be bought (which I suppose I could, but for a lot more than she was offering), met an old friend from the "School" who'd started out giving her the cold shoulder, but was warming up, heard that some of the track's bigwigs were pulling scams with the help of bogus security (which only went to show some people could never have enough), got sent for by a jock in serious hiding who knew for a fact Manny Walker hadn't just drowned, he'd *been* drowned, borrowed

a horse from a "friend" to prove the hidden jock wasn't just
blowing hot air, got beaten up by two of somebody's thugs
in the parking lot of the Grand Union Hotel, got cleaned
up by the nicest guy in Saratoga Springs, and had just now
discovered Fleeting Fancy's new jock was scared witless.

But not so witless he couldn't guide his horse home with
ease and grace in the Fifth at Saratoga.

Holy horsehide. I was sagging on my feet. Not to
mention my back ached like a tooth.

I still had that dinner with Paul Jarrett at 8. I still needed
to keep myself awake until one or two in the morning for a
talk with Alonzo, the elevator operator.

I did what Bogie would of done. I went back to my pink
room in my pink hotel and dreamed lovely pink dreams in
my canopied bed, which thank God, wasn't pink. Not that
I remembered any of 'em. I didn't think Bacall made an
appearance. But I bet Lombard did. She didn't often miss
her scenes in my dreams. I was forever grateful about that.

Dinner with Paul was at a little steak joint off Broadway
on Spring Street. The food wasn't bad. It got better when
Paul turned up in a plain white shirt, and better still when he
paid for the meal. After the day I'd had, Paul paying the tab
took the biscuit. Jarrett was funny and he was clever but he
was tight with a dollar.

"I'm celebrating," he explained.

I didn't like to think about what. I'd bet Mrs. Willingford
had something to do with it, but I didn't ask. I just said that
was fine by me and ordered a brandy. And then I was off
again, telling him all about my glorious day. It amused the
hell out of him, all except the part about me looking like Jim
Mitchum. He stared at me long and hard, then moved his
seat so he could stare long and hard at my dashing profile.
"You know, Sam, that darky wasn't far off."

I didn't like Clay getting called a "darky" but there wasn't
much I could do about it—short of socking a friend in the
nose. So, just to keep the peace, I let that go like I let so
much else go. There was also the fact he hadn't finished what
he was saying.

"You do look a lot like Mitchum. Funny I hadn't noticed

it before."

"And you look like Assault."

Assault, winner of the '46 Kentucky Derby, was no prize for the eye. A bit on the scrawny side, he also limped. Paul took it in the way it was meant, and I went on telling him all about my day until I ran out of steam.

"So what do you think? Accident or murder? With a possible suicide thrown in in the case of McBartle?"

Paul was seldom a serious man. He was serious now. Even more unusual for Paul Jarrett, he was thoughtful. "I'll tell ya, Sam. I don't know what to think. I thought I did. We all thought we did. We all wanted to believe those were three accidents. I can't think of anyone who still doesn't want to think that and not one of 'em'll be happy to hear different. But after what I've heard here, I'm not sure I can think that anymore. You were always the smart kid. You were a reader. Anybody else but you, I'd laugh. But with you, with the Sam Russo who I looked up to—"

That set me back a bit. "You looked up to me?"

"Of course. We all did. Anyways, anybody else but you and I'd tell you to go soak your head. But now, I just don't know. And there's a jock who's hiding?"

"Hell yes."

"One of mine?"

"No."

"If he was, I'd like to think he'd come to me with something like this. I'm supposed to look out for my guys. So you being this licensed private investigator and all, what're you gonna do now? What's your plan?"

How could I tell Paul I had no idea? He looked up to me? He thought I knew what I was doing? People thinking things like that are what made a man a success. If I wanted to be a success as a PI, I had to act like Bogie and *be* a PI. So I gave him what I hoped was a cagey look, and said, "Got an idea I'm following up. I'll know more after that."

Paul held up his glass.

"Here's to the great Sam Russo. The man who's going to save Saratoga!"

I held up my own glass.

"Thanks, Paul."

We clicked glasses and smiled. I felt like an idiot.

23

It was exactly one a.m. when I walked into the overwhelming lobby of the Grand Union Hotel. With no one there, I could count the chandeliers, the red plush chairs, calculate how much gold was used to paint the ceiling cornices and the forest of pillars, how much travertine marble (if it was travertine; that's just a word I'd heard somewhere referring to expensive rocks) was dug out of the earth so expensive shoe leather—ripped off the backs of cattle or alligators or some other living thing—could trip gaily over it, and imagine how much electricity was used up in one day alone.

The elevators were also clad in embossed gold. There were ten of 'em. Five on one side of a grand staircase leading up from the four acre entrance, and five on the other side. Elevator number 9 was on the left. The doors to every one but 9 were closed.

I climbed the staircase. Still not a soul around. I could of stolen the gladioli right out of their vases. The vases, being as big as I was, would of been more difficult.

I once knew a guy, a great guy, and a hell of a great talker and great thinker, always had six ideas on the go at once. This friend had two friends not near as great in any way—but just as crazy. One sunny afternoon, dressed up as delivery men, they walked with complete confidence into the lobby of the Fairmont Hotel in San Francisco, that really ritzy joint on top of some hill called Nob (the name of which I shall not comment on), strolled right up to the reception desk, whereupon the great guy I knew said: "We've come to collect the carpet." He'd pointed at his delivery outfit, "Cleaners, that's us." "Oh," said the sweet young thing manning the desk, and then watched as they rolled up a Persian carpet worth thousands and walked out with it.

Good thing I wasn't like Lino. I never wanted to be a cop or I might of had to do something about my friend. As a PI, I could turn a blind eye unless I was paid to open it.

"Psst!"

Car number 9 was open but empty. But a few feet away and across the wide hallway, stood a decorative glazed jar. Behind that crouched what had to be Alonzo. Alonzo was as black as Black Beauty. He had the body of a ten year old but the face of someone pushing fifty. I liked him immediately. Probably because Thomas Clay Jefferson liked him.

Good thing when we were both behind the jar, there was room to spare. It also had the advantage of Alonzo being able to keep a close eye on car number 9.

First thing he said was, "Clay says I can trust you."

"Not counting the horses, Clay is my favorite Saratogian."

Alonzo grinned at me, a gold tooth in front shining as brightly as the elevator doors. "Mine too."

"I can't keep you here too long. Clay said to ask you about McBartle who was supposed to have walked out of here in good shape at 3:15 a.m. and never come back."

Alonzo poked his head out from our hidey hole. Obviously seeing no one, he drew it back in.

"He wasn't alone."

"Then why did you say he was?"

"Anyone ever threaten your family?"

"No."

"Well, there you go. I only have a wife, but a wife is enough. 'Sides, I like her."

"So what really happened?"

"Looked to me like McBartle was drunk or half asleep or maybe drugged. One or the other of those. And there was this guy holding him up on one side. The big guy was talkin' to him like he could talk back— "

"Big? Like in big or like in real big?"

"Well, seemed to me he was pretty big. And maybe tall. Of course I'm not too big and neither was Mr. McBartle, but I still think he was big. Heck, maybe he was only just large. Anyways, I saw right off the rider fella, he couldn't say nuthin'. So like that, they walked out of that side door over there. It goes to the parking lot and only the valets use it, never the guests. The guests get their cars brought to them out front."

I thought about what he'd said.

"You think McBartle was alive at the time?"

"Yes, sir! He was droolin' and makin' these noises. Anyways, the big guy handed me a sawbuck— "

"Whoa. A lot of dough, ten bucks."

"You better believe it. And when he did, he made a remark about my family. Couldn't miss his meaning. No sir! Clear as a siren. So until now, I ain't said a word. But Clay, he convinced me not sayin' nuthin' was wrong."

"You know who the man was?"

"Nope. Never saw 'im before or since. Or if I did, I din't know it. He kept his hat down way low over his face."

"But you think he was a big guy, right?"

"Well, yeah. Like I said, pretty big. I don't mean a giant or nuthin'. Or a fat guy. Just taller than your average customer. Also strong and steady on his feet. But I did notice one thing."

As a PI, I admit that excited me. A tattoo? A scar? Green hair?

"His shoes. I never saw a pair like 'em."

"What about them?"

"Well, I'll tell ya. If I ever saw 'em again, even half a block away, I'd know 'em."

My heart sank. All that might mean was he was hired talent and was long since back on Broadway playing Macbeth. Or, considering the shoes, Lady Macbeth.

I went back to my soft bed in my pink room in my pink hotel and slept like one of those dead jockeys.

The amazing thing was I woke up not only with the sun, but with an idea. It was the same idea I'd had before I went to sleep, but there were more pieces to find places for, and more of a pattern was beginning to show.

For instance, a pair of unusual shoes.

A shower, a shave, a real breakfast, and Sam Russo, Private Eye, was off to the races.

I was going to spend the whole day there. I might even get in a few bets while I worked on my bona fide idea.

My kidney even felt better. Barely noticed it. Creampuffs, those guys. Real talent and I'd of been pissing red and groaning every step I took.

24

Someone took Manny Walker for a midnight horse ride,
so drunk he probably never woke up, and drowned him in
one of the lakes near the track. Someone drugged Matthew
Mark McBartle and then somehow got it to look like he'd
driven his car accidently into a tree. Someone ruined Babe
Duffy's lunch.

Whoever that someone was rid the world of three young
promising jockeys. Why? There's always a reason for the
things people do, good and bad. Sometimes the reason
makes no sense at all to the usual joe. When the usual joe
does something stupid or bad or both, it's usually for money
or to get rid of the wife (or hubby) or to shut someone else
up. But sometimes it's so personal, only Mister and Florence
Zawadzki, plus their personal god, understood the whys and
wherefores of what they did. The Zawadskis thought killing
a lot of kids for a lot of years, kids they were paid to take care
of, made perfect sense, and as far as I knew, from their cells
in Sing Sing and Bedford Hills, they still did.

But most of the time it makes perfect sense to everyone,
once you know what it is. That was my job. Figure out why
a thing was done, and you're bound to work out who did it.

I could hear Bogie saying that now, lisp and all.

OK. So once I'd eliminated the track itself—star horses
and star jockeys were their bread and butter, it made no
sense to get rid of either—that left Mrs. Willingford. But
to imagine a woman knocking off jocks didn't sit well. She
may have resented the brush-off, but that much? The worst
she'd do was keep the kids off her husband's horses. Then
there was the guy Alonzo spoke of, the one who got out of
the elevator with McBartle so he could take him for his long
last ride. Would she have risked hiring someone?

Didn't think so.

Who wants a jockey out of the picture? Like *The Shadow*,
Sam Russo, hero of the Staten Island Pokey for Tiny Tots,
knows. Who else but another jock? Get rid of the ones with
promise and what happens? Less competition. A mount
in Saratoga race track's most prestigious race: the Travers
Stakes. The Travers was named for the man who was the
first president of the old Saratoga Racing Association and
whose fine horse, Kentucky, won its first running. That was
a long time back: 1864. Kentucky was by Lexington, one
of the greatest racehorses in American history as well as the
greatest stud. Of the first fifteen Travers, nine of them were
won by a son or a daughter of Lexington. Hidden away at the
age of fifteen to keep him from getting stolen by either side
in the Civil War, by then he was already blind. Not seeing a
damn thing didn't put a dent in his efforts to keep making
little Lexingtons.

If there's one horse I would of liked to feed peppermints
to, it was the "Blind Hero of Woodburn."

Enough of that.

Someone built like a jockey: wiry, thin, short, as strong
as the horses they rode, didn't fit Alonzo's description of
the man who led McBartle out of the Grand Union Hotel
elevator. The guy he described sounded more like a middle-
weight boxer than a jockey.

But that was a piece I'd begun to think was slotting into
place. I was sure I was getting somewhere. Actually, I wasn't
sure of anything, but since I couldn't yet think of anything
else, I was playing the hand I held.

Saratoga's racetrack was packed. But I could go where I
wanted to go, sit anywhere, stand anywhere, listen to anyone.
I was on a job here.

I went straight to the jockey's dressing room. For the
time being, I ignored Alonzo's description—who knew?
Maybe if the guy knew someone might spot him, he wore
stilts. Anyway, if a jock was the culprit, that's where he'd be.
Coming and going from race to race to race, as many as he
could get mounts in.

Everyone was at the track. From jocks to agents to
owners to trainers, they knew who I was and why I was

there. I was looking at 'em all. And they were looking at me. Even Hank Hanson, an old friend and the track vet, was around, looking at a cut over Toby Tyrrell's eye. It was a fresh cut so it must of just happened in the last race.

Hadn't said hello to Hank yet; I made a mental note to do that and got back to work.

If "everyone" included the killer, then he'd be sure to get a little nervous me hanging around, watching the races, talking with people. That's what I hoped to see. Someone acting guilty.

I had a few reasons made me think I'd make a decent PI. One of 'em was because I thought I knew what guilty looked like. I'd seen it enough hanging around with Lino Morelli. He didn't seem to notice, but I did. The eyes, the mouth, the body language. Reading those library books a few days back told me Hercule Poirot used the same methods. But he was just a funny little man made up by an ugly English dame—one smart cookie of an ugly English dame, I had to give her that.

Sometimes the guilt had nothing to do with what I was looking for, and sometimes it did. I was right more often than I was wrong.

Me and Paul, we'd worked out a little scene. We'd have what should look like a private conversation during the prep for the second race. I was going to tell Paul what I'd told him at dinner. Without all the details, of course, but the idea was to rehash what we'd said over steak and salad.

If that didn't spook anyone, I'd—well, I'd have to think of something else. With Lino, I had this knack of coming up with a new idea when some old idea went bust. He counted on that, not having an idea himself. For a minute there, I worried that maybe off the Isle of Staten in the middle of my own case, the knack would desert me. But I brushed that aside like Bogie brushed aside other people's wise cracks.

Paul Jarrett showed up right on time. He talked to one of the jocks—one he agented—he talked to George Labold. Funny, I hadn't noticed before; Paul stood the same height as George. Anyway, they were probably making bet on whose jock would win the next race. Paul talked to an owner, one of

those excited types who got in everyone's hair but he had to
tolerate the guy. Owners paid the bills. They got tolerated.
He checked on some tack. He had a word with a trainer,
must of trained a horse one of his lads was riding. And then
he pretended to notice me. I'd been sitting on a chair by a
window smoking for over an hour. I'd also been doing a lot
of staring. First at one jock, then at another. Now and then
at Labold which made him all of a sudden busy at the far
side of the room. The din was incredible. Jocks in and out,
showering from crossing the finish line last or first, didn't
matter, they were covered with dirt and sweat. Jocks using
the one telephone to call in bets on other races, other sports.
Jocks pushing each other around for bad riding, deliberate
or otherwise. Jocks yelling at their agents. Lockers opening
and closing and always loud. Every now and then a jock
tried looking at me in a way I wasn't supposed to notice. I
noticed. I'd also been thinking. This wasn't the greatest idea
in the world, and it wasn't the worst. But while I'd been
sitting there acting like I knew something no one else knew,
I'd had another idea. This idea was a good one. A really
good one. If the police had taken any of this seriously from
the beginning, some bright spark would already of thought
of it, and then followed it up. But they weren't taking it
seriously so even if it had been thought of, it hadn't gotten
any further.

    This idea was mine. I'd get to it as soon as I'd played the
scene Paul and I arranged.

    Soon as I pretended to see him, I acted like I'd been
waiting for him. He acted like he was surprised I was
waiting for him. We talked. Not too close to our audience
and not too far away. At the right moment, I said as loudly
as I could without coming off like a bad actor in a bad play:
"They weren't accidents, Paul, and they weren't suicides."

    Paul's surprise was priceless. A kind of a W. C. Fields
double take. "Not accidents? But I thought— "

    "You thought wrong."

    "So if they weren't acci... ?"

    "They were murders. All three of 'em."

    You couldn't hear a pin drop. But then, who could hear a

pin drop? But you definitely couldn't hear the racket I'd been listening to for over an hour because the racket had stopped like a car hitting a tree. I looked at the room, quickly, before every single one of 'em could get his game face back on. The only face in the room that looked anything but shocked and surprised was the angelic Tyrone Power-ish face of Toby Tyrrell. Tyrrell, who'd been wiping his newly bandaged eye with a hand towel, looked exactly like this young fellow Lino once collared for embezzlement. Scared, humiliated, slightly witless, and cornered.

Dammit.

Paul saw what I saw. I couldn't put my finger on what was written all over Paul Jarrett's face—but it didn't spell pleased.

It also messed a little with my great idea, so I wasn't pleased either. But hey, I'd figure it out. Still lengths behind at the clubhouse turn, I was one hell of a closer. At least I was around Lino. Lino Morelli was so dumb he was smart and when he got smart, I noticed even if he didn't.

Not being around Lino and the smart things he'd trip over, I hoped I still had it.

25

I stole something before Paul and I left the dressing room after the fourth race. Tucked it under the light cotton jacket I wore. A Private Eye does a lot of things. He lies. He steals. He pretends to be someone he's not. He does what he has to do, except murder. Killing in self defense doesn't count. We all do that. I needed my little theft. Without it, the good idea I'd had sitting around the jockey's dressing room waiting to go through my charade with Paul, wouldn't work. With it, my good idea got my blood up.

As a born snoop, good ideas made my heart race as well as my mind. Images were flashing through so fast I could barely keep up. I didn't know where Paul was going, and I didn't care. I knew where I was going.

I got waylaid in an empty corridor by the grim face of Marshall Hutsell. The rest of him was there too. Plus hat. Just for the record, he was a big man.

"You," he said, "a word."

"Well, maybe just one—I'm in a hurry here."

"Enough with the wise stuff. I got a message for you."

"A message? For me?" I thought of batting my eyelashes but why waste time?

"Management says you're on the wrong track."

"Nice message. On the wrong track. That's a good one."

"Nobody's paying for lip, Russo. They're paying for results."

"They also paying for extras on the set?"

"What's that mean?"

"You know, guys with special talents. Like low blows in parking lots."

"What the hell are you yacking about? Guys like you make me sick. Just keep your nose pointed in the right direction."

I gave him my best wartime salute which only made him grimmer. I got to leave first. That felt good.

My way off the track took me back of a set of bleachers built there for the overflow Saratoga race track expected for their biggest draws: the Whitney Handicap and the Travers Stakes.

Turning a corner, head down, while under it my mind danced a mad excited jig, I came to a sudden and complete halt.

My day was full of Paul Jarrett. He was half the length of the bleachers away and he wasn't alone. There were three toughs surrounding him and not one of 'em looked friendly or like my toughs from the day before. Two had hold of Paul's arms, the third stood in front, jabbing him in the gut. Paul could take a punch—he'd taken plenty back in our old school days, some of 'em meant for me. He could take the jabbing, I wasn't worried about that. I wasn't too worried about things getting out of hand either. This time my gun wasn't back at the hotel. It was snug and safe, right in my pocket. My real worry was why was Paul getting the treatment?

Being in the war taught me some stuff. In the heat of the moment I forgot one of 'em—the advantage of surprise. I yelled: "Hey!"

All four heads turned my way. All four and their cheap suits were startled.

Paul looked relieved. And something else—but things were going way too fast to figure exactly what.

I was walking towards them, more like trotting, and I had my hand in my pocket making sure they got the point I wasn't some schmuck butting in where he wasn't wanted.

"Knock it off," I yelled, "and do it now!"

I'd showed up so fast and so unexpected no one even thought to move; they just stood there, like ancient statues of gone-to-seed gladiators, watching me come.

What a trio. Slow wasn't the word. If I'd hired 'em, I'd of already fired 'em. They let me get close enough to pull my gun. They let me aim it at the forehead of the guy who'd been doing the jabbing.

Holding the gun, I sounded calmer than I felt, a lot calmer. "We all know I haven't got time to shoot every one of you, but I do have time to shoot one. So I choose… you."

The thug with the .38 caliber gun muzzle up against his forehead would of liked to grin. He'd of liked to impress the other two thugs. Trouble was, he did.

He said, "What's your name, meatball?"

"Sam Spade."

"I won't forget that."

"It's a name to remember. I always do."

"What's this to do with you? You know this jerk?"

"This jerk is practically my brother."

"Like I'm so scared. I ain't scared of you."

"I can tell. We can all tell, can't we, boys?"

For that, I got a hint of a smile from one of the jerks holding Paul.

"Let 'em go, boys," said the jerk with the muzzle of a gun held against his forehead. To me he snarled, "But don't think this is over. This ain't over until I says it's over."

I wasn't the only one watching the movies. I liked to think I watched better stuff.

The two mopes let Paul go, each releasing their grip at the same time. And then all three walked away, the one who'd done the jabbing and the talking, way in front. All three remembered to swagger.

When they'd got far enough, I turned to Paul. I was hanging on to what was left of my own swagger with my teeth. Truth was, I'd been scared. I bet even Bogie would of had a nasty moment. Would I have shot the dumb gunsel? I'd shot a lot of guys, all in the name of freedom, but shoot a guy point blank?

I don't think I'd of shot him.

"OK. What was that all about?"

Paul shrugged his shoulders. His ears were the deep pink of the petunias in my pastel pink boxes at my pink-all-over hotel.

"Same old, same old, right, Paul? Gambling debts?"

"Same old is right. As for same old, you sure are the

same old Sam. That was the nicest play I ever saw."

"Sure. And you're doing my laundry. How much do you owe the bookie they work for?"

Paul didn't pretend not to understand. "A grand, more or less."

"A thousand bucks! My great Aunt Hilda, Jarrett! Where the hell are you going to get a thousand bucks?"

"Now there's the big question. The one I've been chewing on for some time."

"Guys like that kill guys like you for dough like that."

"How true."

"So they're going to kill you?"

"That about says it all."

"In that case, do I buy flowers now or do you have a plan?"

Paul smiled his charming Paul smile. "Well, Fleeting Fancy could win the Travers."

"That's your plan? Dumping what's left of your dough on a horse race?"

"Not exactly. But sort of, yep, that's most of my plan."

"Anything can happen in a horse race. The best horse doesn't always win. The worst horse can somehow come home."

"Another true thing. Which means I have to have a Plan B."

"Which is?"

"Running away."

"Better plan, Paul. But there goes your career in the horse racing business."

"Sadly, also true."

I looked at him. What could I say? Paul Jarrett was in another fine mess. He was also taking it like he took stuff when we were kids. As if it was all a big joke.

"It seems to me," he said, "this calls for a drink."

"Sorry, Paul. I have a date with a dog."

That wiped the stupid smile off his face. Jarrett's goofy grin was replaced by a mix of surprise and confusion—which did me a world of good.

It slowed my heart which was racing faster than Phar Lap ever since I turned that corner behind the bleachers.

26

I had something else to borrow—well, OK, steal—before I followed through with my big idea. This item wouldn't be so easy to clip as the first one was, but it wouldn't be that hard.

I hoped.

I was back from the track and in the Grand Union Bar on Broadway. This time, I was in luck. Mrs. Willingford wasn't posing anywhere—I really didn't want Mrs. Willingford watching me work—but Hollie Hayes was.

Hollie was propped on the same bar stool at the same bar doing exactly what he'd been doing the last time I saw him: drinking out of a coffee cup like it was still Prohibition. He was drinking heavily. A winning ticket. All I had to do was get close enough to get my hands on anything he'd touched. Bookended by fellow drunks, neither of which looked like a pal, I waited in a huge green chair half hidden by one of those potted palms that only lived in hotel lobbies. If I'd been a botanist instead of a PI, I'd study those things. Make a career out of 'em. Plants that only lived in lobbies and bathrooms. I was sure to fascinate dozens in the field of indoor plant life.

It took half an hour of plant watching until one of the drunks paid his bill, tipped his hat to the bartender but gave the guy no actual tip—that earned him a well deserved sneer—and wove his way to the men's room. I was on his empty stool faster than Eddie Arcaro on a stakes winning horse.

Hollie Hayes hadn't lost his dress sense just because he'd lost his two best jockeys. He remained as colorful as a kid's birthday party. His nose hadn't grown any longer but it was some nose. Jimmy Durante should of sued.

I'd decided to try for a conversation. What could he do?

Shoot me? I'd had enough of that to last this entire case.

I ordered the usual, and while waiting, pretended I suddenly recognized him. I was trying for that whole wow, gee whizz, well I'll be darned, bobby sox fan thing, without being obnoxious about it—which was harder than I thought it would be. Turns out, it was impossible. Fans are obnoxious. That's who they are. I should of tried being just another drunk, but it was too late because I'd already practically sung out as I sat: "Hollie Hayes!"

Hollie swung that face with its award winning nose round, focused on my nose (pathetic by comparison), and said, "Who wants to know?"

"Name's Sam Russo. Big fan."

"Of what?"

"You."

"What the hell for? All I do is handle jockeys. Dead jockeys."

"Uh. Right."

My prize for this embarrassing exchange lay on the bar in front of both of us. A pair of Hollie's gloves, which only Hollie would wear on a hot summer's day in Saratoga Springs. They were a light weight cotton, colored robin's egg blue, which clashed well with the lime green of his shirt and the orange and yellow checks of his jacket.

I wanted one of those blue gloves. At the same time I didn't want anyone to see me take it. Especially Hollie Hayes. I ordered a double, threw it back, and ordered another. I may have begun as a fan but I could finish as a drunk.

Just sitting there drinking while he drank wasn't going to get me a glove. Hollie was bound to ask what the hell I thought I was doing sliding his personal property off the bar. If I "accidently" knocked one off, he'd expect it back. There was also the bartender. The place wasn't crowded. Other than shining glasses and topping up the three drunks in front of him: Hollie, the other guy, and me, he didn't have a lot to do. He was sure to spot me clipping the glove.

Only a fan trying for a souvenir, I'd still get nailed.

I suddenly noticed it. A handkerchief in Hollie's pants pocket. Rose colored. Gorgeous. Just perfect. What could go better with orange and yellow?

Someone once told me most men were color blind. I didn't doubt it for a minute. It explained Hollie's dress sense. Hollie was some kind of male. He was color blind. Who'd dress the way Hollie dressed on purpose?

Anyways, he was a drunk. Sam Russo was a drunk. The other guy was a drunk. What do drunks do besides drink? They fall over. I fell over. Hollie Hayes, on the stool next to mine, kept me from landing on my ass by not falling over with me. He got a fast hold on the brass rim of the bar top and held on. Me, I grasped his sleeve, his waist, his entire body, and apologizing like the mad drunken fan I was, I slipped that rosy red cloth out of his pants pocket deep into mine, and *then* I let myself slide sideways off the stool. Landed on my knees in the bar of the Grand Union Hotel, which hurt like hell, picked myself up, and tottered off as fast as my drunken fan's legs and my cracked knees and my reawakened kidney could carry me.

No cry of outrage from Hollie was such a lovely lack of sound I hummed myself out the front door, knees or no knees.

I stood on the steps of the biggest hotel in New York State, breathing deep to clear my head, thinking: a PI's life wasn't girls, guns and guts. It was humiliating. What was I thinking? There was now a bartender who thought I was a bigger drunk than Hollie Hayes. There were two drunks going home glad they weren't as sloppy as me.

Did Bogie ever go through this? It helped to remember the scene in *The Big Sleep* where he flipped up the brim of his hat, slipped on a pair of thick black rimmed glasses, lisped more than he usually did, and went through an entire pansy routine in what pretended to be a bookstore.

I felt a lot better. I was now a drunk, but I wasn't a pansy.

Sucking in the fine Saratoga air, remembering I didn't owe a bookie a single dime, and feeling the rosy rag in my coat pocket, I got myself feeling just fine.

For this one moment, life was pure silk.

27

I was looking for Babe Duffy's dog.

Before I followed up on my fine idea, one worthy of Sam Spade or Philip Marlowe (maybe even a better idea; I loved both those guys, but their cases were never long on sleuthing), I'd checked around.

Jane was some sort of hunting dog from Africa. I figured Babe named her Jane because it was the only African word he knew: as in "Me Tarzan, you Jane." Whenever Babe was in town he stayed at the farm of a Thoroughbred breeder about nine miles southeast of the city of Saratoga. The breeder's place was called Up and Down Hill Farm. It was where Jane lived until they found her a home.

Trouble with dogs like Jane, they were a one-man-dog and no one at Up and Down Hill suited Jane's taste.

I'd gotten all this from the farm manager. My story when I called this guy was I'd met Babe a few months before he'd died, and I really liked his dog. Then I heard about his senseless accident. So I'd wondered: perhaps Jane would like me?

Jane must of been a real pip of a pet. I could tell Roland the farm manager couldn't get me out there fast enough. The idea was to fool me into taking her away—permanently.

I stood in front of the stallion barn while Babe's dog walked all around me, her African head with its African nose sniffing my ankles, her long African tail tightly curled over her short back. Any minute I expected her to lower her African ass and piss on my Staten Island shoes.

"She likes you," said Roland.

I said, "How can you tell?"

I knew what he wanted to say. I knew he was itching to say it. Because she hasn't bitten you yet. But he couldn't. He wanted rid of the dog too bad.

"Well look at her. You got her attention."

"She doesn't bite, does she?"

"Bite? That dog?"

I didn't care who she bit. I only wanted Babe's dog to get in the car I'd come in. I didn't want her around for long. Just long enough to help me do what I needed to do.

The car was a deep green 1946 Buick sedan. The guys who'd hired me and hadn't fired me yet, provided the Buick.

I'd survived Hutsell's "warning." It didn't take much to know the goons who beat the crap out of me in the parking lot of the Grand Union Hotel were Hutsell's goons, and Marshall Hutsell was a goon for whoever was paying the tab. The beating was his way of reminding me I was only there for show, there were no cases to solve.

Hutsell was too quick on the draw. If he'd left me alone, I could of wound up agreeing. But the beating plus this, that, and the other, changed my way of looking at things. I didn't agree. And every hour that passed, I agreed even less.

In Saratoga, from getting off the train 'til now, Hutsell had done all the talking. Hutsell got me what I wanted when I asked for it—like an up-to-the-minute list of every horse, trainer, owner, and jockey at the track.

When I got canned, Hutsell would be the guy telling me.

But until then, I was doing my job.

Jane, who had a squint on her like she'd stared at the sun, didn't like me. A coupla sniffs and that was it. Didn't come near me again. But she liked me more than she liked Roland the farm manager. Him, she yodeled at. You'd think a yodel couldn't sound scary? Think again.

She really hated the horse being led out of the barn when I was trying to sound like a friend of Babe Duffy's. Big and black and beautiful, his hot walker called him Walking Tall but Roland called him Bob. Faster than Bob probably ran, Jane went for his back left hock. I had to hand it to Roland, he was also speedy. He kicked Jane clear across the drive and into a bush before Bob had a chance to. Jane was up on her feet and coming again when I opened the Buick door and called to her. Who knows about dogs? Not me. I was as surprised as Roland when she chose the Buick instead of Bob. Damned if she didn't launch herself into the front passenger seat, then sit there staring out through the windshield.

Roland shrugged his shoulders. I shrugged mine. Bob snorted. The hotwalker spat on the ground.

I turned to tell Roland I was taking Babe's dog for a spin, see if we got along. But the man was already walking away. He had a little spring in his step. I knew what he was thinking. He was thinking, God bless America, there goes that damn dog. He was wrong. I was working on my great idea and when I'd done that, Jane was coming back to Up and Down Hill Farm.

Sorry, I'd say, wrong dog. Not a good fit.

Jane and I drove all the way to Babe's last picnic spot without a yodel between us. I stared out the windshield so I could tell where we were going. She stared out the windshield for her own reasons. But passing through a gate that led to a certain mineral springs, one of her short perky ears cocked up. Just one. At the same time, her upper lip curled, exposing fine white teeth.

I parked, got out, went round to her side of the car, and opened her door. I'd expected her to leap outside but it didn't happen. What happened was exactly nothing. Jane sat in the car. She didn't even turn her head to look at me. So I dug Hollie's rose colored hanky out of my pocket.

My thinking went like this. Hollie Hughes managed two of the dead jocks. This could mean their smell should still be on him. That in itself wouldn't matter, but if Hollie had been around their murderer, or if Hollie were their murderer (and therefore faking his grief; I'd worry later about *why* Hollie would kill his own living), Jane would go nuts.

"Here, girl. Sniff this. You know about this?"

I got a response. It was slow, but it was something. Jane lay down. Lying down, she looked like the Sphinx before one of Napoleon's men blew most of its face off.

I rummaged around in my other pocket for what I'd taken from the jock's room back at the track: the cloth used to wipe the blood off Toby Tyrrell's face. It'd been tossed on the floor for some other poor sap to clean up.

Toby got the mount on Fleeting Fancy. Maybe he killed for it?

The moment I stuck Toby's cloth under her nose, Jane sailed from the car in one balletic movement, and raced away, headed straight for the spot where Babe Duffy's body'd spent two days deader than a dead heat. Never leaving his side sat his African dog Jane. On guard. Mourning.

Jane was a red and white streak far ahead, disappearing round a bend on the wooded path I'd meant to follow. When I caught up, she was sitting on a huge golden slide of hardened minerals. The smell of sulfur was as strong as the smell of Staten Island's breweries. Both took getting used to.

Inhaling sulfur made Jane wrinkle her useful doggy nose. Added to her wrinkled forehead, she was something to look at. But not approach. I hadn't forgotten the stallion.

Babe died on a rock. He'd been sitting on a huge translucent yellow rock with his faithful dog Jane, eating a ham sandwich. And then what happened? Jane knew. She'd watched the whole thing. Had she taken a bite out of someone? After the scene with the stallion, I knew she would of tried. But did she succeed?

One thing I did know: if she saw whoever it was again, she'd know it and she'd react—and although I didn't think a fierce dog's fearsome animosity would mean much to the cops or the courts, I'd know who my culprit was. Once I knew that, I also knew that if it took me forever, I'd find something, anything, that proved it. In my world, killing three good jocks was a huge no-no, as bad as killing a horse.

I pulled Hollie's hanky out of my pocket once more, held it up to her. She still ignored it. So I tried Toby's cloth again. This time she cocked both ears and jumped, first to race up a leaf scattered path that arrived at the golden rock from a different direction, then to run around the rock, yodeling.

I guessed all the bark had long ago been bred out of a dog like Jane, but not the voice. She could yodel, she could make gurgling noises deep in her throat, and her version of a whine was tuneful.

The killer arrived from the other path. Using it, either

he (or the long shot she), would of been heard coming by both dog and man. The crunch and crinkle of leaves would give him away. But Babe stayed on his rock. What could that mean? That it was just someone passing by and Babe had no reason to worry? Or that Babe knew who was coming and still had no reason to worry—or so he thought?

Jane wasn't going back to Up and Down Hill Farm quite yet. First she was going for another ride.

28

Saratoga's racing season was short. So was my employment. It covered a couple of weeks. I'd already used up plenty of that time.

This day's racing was over. All over the better part of town, the well heeled and the well connected were deep in a bottle of this or that. They were stuffing their faces with what I'd heard 'em call "finger food." That was one of those names that told you exactly why: because they ate it with their fingers. Right now, fingering, chewing, swallowing, slurping, they were yelling in each other's overfed faces about this race or that, this horse or that, this dollar lost or won.

I really felt left out.

Toby Tyrrell was too young for baloney like that. Plus he wasn't famous enough to be feted by those who couldn't ride or train or do much of anything with a horse but own it. So where would he be? Home most likely. And home for now was the track where the jocks dossed for the season. All except those like the once mighty Matthew Mark McBartle. Or the now terrified Mash Mooney.

Jane and I got through the closed gate with ease: a wave of the hand, a yodel. I parked the Buick. By now Jane was talking to me more than Lino used to talk to me. I guessed I was listening to a constant harangue of ancient Egyptian. If I knew her much longer, one of us was going to have to learn English or Egyptian. Probably me. I suspected her command of her tongue was better than my command of mine. I blamed the great education I got at the Staten Island Home for Left Over Kids. That I could string together any kind of sentence came from listening to Mister's radio and reading whatever I could get my hands on—not a bad haul, now I recall, since a handful of kids had visitors and some of

the visitors brought books, not to mention a castoff or two
from a charity or two.

Thinking about it, why weren't there any teachers?
Thinking about it some more: what a stupid question.
Because Mr. & Mrs. Zawadzki ran the place, that's why.

Like all the other interesting things going on where I grew
up, the State of New York seldom got round to noticing.

No one was asleep at the jockeys' "house." Jocks were
lying back on their bunks, some smoking, some drinking,
some doing both. In a corner, some played cards. Jocks were
listening to the radio—Spike Jones was adding his personal
touch to *The William Tell Overture*. Two or three were trying
to read. One was reading an actual book. I tried to catch
the title but he'd covered it with paper from a brown paper
bag. Toby, clear across the room, was shaving. Shaving what
I didn't know. He was sixteen. Maybe he was practicing, a
man among men.

Jane saw him or smelt him or whatever she did—and
she was gone. Dodging bunks and hands and calls of "Jane!",
"Hey! That's Babe's dog, Jane!" making her way right for
him.

I was left flat-footed. I'd never get there before she did.
By the time I saw Toby Tyrrell again, he could be pulp.

Was my case solved? Did a kid eager for fame kill off his
rivals? If so, I suddenly wasn't so happy with the PI game. I
hated what he'd done and why he'd done it, if he'd done it.
If he'd done it, I hated taking him down.

But Jane didn't jump him. She didn't growl and she
didn't snarl. She didn't bare her teeth to bite. No teeth, no
claws, just nose—almost caused him to cut his own throat
with the straight edge.

Jane was breathing him in, inch by inch, like a cop would
all over a piece of prize evidence. And all the time, she was
talking to him.

I swear I understood her. Jane was saying, "You know
what happened to Babe? You know where the killer is?"

"Jesus, doggie. Get down!" was all Toby got out before
Jane caught another scent and was gone, belly to the floor,
nose to the floorboards, here, there, everywhere. And then

she stopped, her tail uncurled like a stump on her rump, and with that she made a kind of strangled oops! noise and was streaking back through the scrambling jocks and out a back door. Me, I was right after her. Damn, but dogs, even small dogs, could move when they wanted to.

The back door took us into an alley between the horse barns. The heads of curious horses appeared over doors, the thud of hooves hit the walls as one or another woke up. Jane was mad for what she was smelling. And I was mad not to lose her. But I did. She got round a corner before I was halfway down a row, and when I turned that same corner, she was gone. I tried calling her name. Nothing. So I walked slowly down a new row with new horses, some with name tags over their doors any other time I'd be proud to stand near. But no time. I kept going, glancing down every new turn, left and right.

Finally, there she was, sitting on her neat little butt, her upright ears loose on her head, her tail flat on the ground, her eyes full of dejected guilt.

I saw why. She'd lost the scent when it reached a huge pile of fresh horse shit. That much shit and even a dog like Jane lost her way.

She turned to look up at me, gave out a series of melodic yodels. If I'd ever heard grief, I was hearing it now.

OK. So the killer of at least Babe Duffy—and if Babe, then two to one also the killer of McBartle and Walker—was someone who came to the track. He (or she) wasn't a handicapper or a regular paying customer. He was a horseman: an owner, a trainer, a grounds-man, a hot-walker, someone who belonged behind the scenes on a daily basis. Probably not a jockey.

Not being a jock made me feel better. I didn't want a jock killing jocks. In the sport I loved, those I loved best—after the horses—were the jockeys.

There was a discreet little sign next to the spiked iron gate of the pink hotel. Shaded by petunias, it said: *No Pets. Thank you for your understanding.*

Understanding but not giving a shit, I wrapped Jane up

in the car blanket and smuggled her into my room. A little water in a saucer, a can of dog food I'd bought at a corner store dumped into a decorative bowl (had to dump the flowers out, float 'em in a skillet I found in my kitchenette), and she was set for the night.

Then I was back out the door and on the prowl.

I admitted it if only to myself. That great gumshoe, Sam Russo, needed to talk to someone.

29

Fifteen minutes of slow walking, hat on the back of my head, hands shoved in my pants pockets, and once again packing heat, I was back in the Grand Union Hotel. Specifically I was back in the opulent gents of the Grand Union Hotel with the only sane person I'd met in Saratoga Springs. Or, for that matter, pretty much anywhere else. In the world I knew, sanity was a rare thing, Most people acted sane, doing their best to get through the average man's average day. But under the skull they were a stew of fruit and nuts.

That included yours truly.

If nothing else, I'm a quick study. I stopped going anywhere in Saratoga Springs without a gun.

Thomas Clay Jefferson was wearing what he'd worn the last time I saw him: his Grand Union Hotel uniform. On me, I'd look like Haile Selassie on one of his over-dressed days. On Clay, it looked just fine. It helped he'd left off the feathered hat and the bogus medals.

If I'd made any real headway on my first real case, you couldn't prove it by me. S'why I was seeking out the only person besides Paul I felt I could talk to. Talking to myself was getting confusing. Talking to Jane maybe didn't confuse her, but listening to her talk to me was turning into a headache. She talked more than Walter Winchell talked, and made about as much sense.

Talking to Clay felt like I was talking to someone like Ghandi—a real crime some pill of a Hindu gunsel'd just shot the fellow. The things people do to each other far far away, like New Jersey for example, didn't really get to me. Ghandi getting mortally plugged did.

All the more reason to value Thomas Clay Jefferson.

He was busy shining some smooth twit's shoes. No

chitchat: Clay was a menial. He was a wall-eyed colored man. A twit like the current twit didn't even see him. The shoes were nothing much either—just your usual pair that could of fed a family of four for a week. Nothing unusual about the twit either. Half the men at the bar could change places and who would know? The man in the chair flipped Clay a nickel, then bounced out of the gents feeling like the soul of generosity. This I noticed by the smile he gave himself passing the full length mirror. Why the mirror smiled back was something for someone like Einstein to figure out. But why it quickly sucked in its belly was something even I could figure out. In a year, maybe two, the guy would be sporting a girdle.

That left me on some sort of horsehair covered couch people perched on when women wore bustles, and Clay on the upright gilded chair he sat on when he wasn't shining shoes.

I'd brought a little something in a hip flask and offered it to him. He took it, but not before checking we were alone.

His swallow was dainty but it took in a lot of hootch. I didn't mind if he drank the whole thing. That's why I brought it.

"Now sir, that was mighty fine bourbon. And I know my bourbon."

"You're welcome, Clay."

I had a lot more to say than that, but couldn't think how to get started. So instead of talking I smoked the Grand Union's free tobacco, although I lit it with my own match. Clay, being Clay, figured I was struggling with my opening line about the same time I did.

"Alfonzo said you talked to him."

"I did."

"He told you about the big man."

"He did."

"Then you know that poor rider didn't take himself for a ride?"

"I do."

"Ah! Have you formed an opinion yet? Come to any conclusions?"

"You want the truth, Clay?"

"'Course I do. Got no interest in anything but."

"I haven't the faintest idea."

"Thought that might be the case."

"Some shamus I am. Not one of those deaths was an accident. I've worked how they were done. I've met a girl, sings like Heidi, who knows who killed Babe. But I don't know why. Motive's everything. Any PI and most cops could tell you that."

One eye closed in deep satisfaction, the other surveying the ceiling, Clay was knocking back another slug of bourbon. With great care he removed a showy hanky from his pocket and with greater care wiped his mouth and then the flask. "This girl you talkin' about— "

"Jane. Babe Duffy's dog. She saw everything. Today she proved whoever it was, it wasn't a jock."

"You malign yourself, sir. You have made much progress. As much as I have."

"You have?"

"I do not spend my life, Mr. Russo, in a jumped-up toilet."

"Right. Sorry."

"Perhaps you know things I do not know, and I perhaps know things you do not know. Get up in that chair and let me shine them shoes. People might wonder otherwise."

For the next half hour, I mostly listened to Clay. His family and his friends were spread out all over the Spa, working in every conceivable job, except of course those offering power and money. What they didn't know wasn't much, although they still didn't know the actual name of the killer. Turns out Clay's family and friends had five major suspects but none pinned down yet.

"And the one they like the most?"

"Well, sir, the one most seem to agree on is a certain employee of the track, a Mr.... "

"Hutsell?"

"The very one. But I imagine that like you, I can't think why he or his employers would want fine young jockeys out of this world."

"You imagine correctly. You'd think they'd want more on the ground. They'd breed 'em like the horses if they could."

"They used to, sir, they used to."

"You're referring to when most jocks were slaves."

"You know your history. I thought you might."

"I try and keep up."

"Now, the one I like the most has to do with Mrs. Willingford."

"Why her?"

"As old as a tale in the good book, sir. Who doesn't think she wants rid of the old man for his money?"

"And how would killing jockeys get rid of the old man? Why not just kill the old man?"

"Well, I been thinkin' on that. First part's easy. Po-lice would right away look to her for the deed. Besides, that old man is so old, he'll be gone on his own soon enough. Second part's where it gets tricky. What if she wanted a certain man who didn't want her? A poor man by her standards but much more to her likin'. If she could make him dependant on her— "

"Having a hard time following your thoughts, Clay."

"As am I. I'm workin' on the idea of making a man need you for his livin'. And if she can get him that way, tie him up tight, why then, he'd be hers."

"You are talking about a particular man, aren't you Clay? One you know."

"Could be. Could be. Now sir, I know that's not much of a reason for killing three young men, but the way I see it is they had to go to get this other man closer. And when it comes to what she wants, I think that woman is as mean as a cat tossed inna well— "

The door to the gents slammed open and in came two gents who might as well of been the one gent who'd left last.

"There you go, sir. All done."

Clay ran his cloth across my over-shined shoes one more time, and turned to smile at the newcomers. His right eye looked at the swell on the right, his left eye looked at me. Either eye, I had no idea what they saw.

"Is there something I can do for you two gentl'men?"

"Is there something he can do, Charlie?"

"What's a cockeyed nigger for, Bert?"

That was the end of that. I went away seething. For one thing, I couldn't just stick around waiting for the two crumbs to leave. For another, if I stuck around I'd plug both of 'em in the foot, one in the left foot and one in the right.

I'd still be risking Clay's job. And he'd be the poor sap to clean it up.

But oh yes, it was hard walking away nice and quiet. It was real hard.

30

In a mood fit for nobody, I walked past the bar of the Grand Union headed for the big front door and home. If I stuck around, no telling what damage I'd do.

But even mad as hell I caught a glimpse of myself in one of the mirrors the Grand Union lobby was full of. The place was like a fun house.

No girdle for me. I couldn't see myself getting fat as a PI. There wasn't enough money in it. But I could see myself getting old real fast. The people you met were those kinds of people.

"Always running away, that's you."

The voice was like ice cream. Cold and sweet at the same time. I had to stop and face her. If I didn't, she'd be right. I'd be running away.

"Something I can do for you, Mrs. Willingford?"

"You? What could you ever do for me?"

"Work up a snappier routine?"

For that I came this close to a slap in the face. I noticed her hands. Mrs. Willingford had hands like the rest of her, beautiful. I thought of Clay's one dollar win bet, the one he'd just put down on Mrs. Willingford's nose. Could she of hauled Walker out of bed, thrown him across the back of a horse, and dumped him in the lake? If she dressed right, wore a disguise, would Alonzo see her as a big guy? Alonzo was small. No telling what he saw big as. Was she strong enough to shove a sandwich down Babe's throat and hold it there until he died? Not on your life. But could she hire someone to do all that? You bet she could.

Why? I wish to hell I'd had time to hear more of Clay's reasoning. More time to talk it over with him. We were bound to get somewhere, even to where he was wrong. But no going back now. For some damn reason, the gents was

suddenly looking popular and for another I had to get away
from anywhere Mrs. Willingford was. That meant out of the
Grand Union Hotel.

I turned my back and walked away. I'd read somewhere
that you never turn your back on a suspect, but the way I was
feeling, I would of turned my back on Billy the Kid.

Walking home took less time than walking to the Grand
Union. I was dog tired. Not so much from what I'd been
doing; I was tired of not knowing why I was doing it, I was
tired of running into closed doors.

When I got back to my own door in the pink hotel, it
was open.

Damn it all to hell. That was a real kick in the head, the
imperfect end to an imperfect day. Jane must of got out.

I went in expecting nothing more than no dog and a hard
night's sleep. What I got almost killed me. It sure killed
Jane.

I'd never met my mother, never seen a photograph. All
the same I had a picture in my head, a girl I'd made up, one
I'd see now and then when I thought about her. I saw her
now. Like my mother, my borrowed dog hadn't left at all.
Someone'd paid a call while I was out messing around in the
can of the Grand Union Hotel.

My place was torn to pieces. Dishes smashed on the floor,
forks and spoons and knives scattered from one baseboard to
another. Whoever showed up met Jane. Meeting Jane must
of been one hell of a nasty surprise. She'd gone for him with
everything she had—and he'd fought back.

Whatever she did to the guy, however bad it was, Jane
lost in the end. She was lying on her side, half in and half
out of the bathroom, stabbed I don't know how many times,
blood all over her and most of the room.

The knife was one of mine. I mean it was one of the
steak knives that belonged in the kitchenette. Now it was
lying on the floor where she was lying. Looked like it was
dropped there, like whenever whoever got through doing
such a damned cowardly thing, he just let it go, let it land
where it would.

But oh, for such a small dog, there was so much blood.

Someone killed my dog. She *was* my dog. No one else wanted her. Not even me, but somehow I'd known ever since I saw the grief in her eyes we were stuck with each other.

Thinking I'd sit for a minute, thinking my heart would slow down, thinking I could stop thinking and maybe even stop feeling, I missed the end of the bed. Clutching the thing for balance, I cursed, and when I cursed, I heard the smallest sound, a hint of a yodel. It was coming from over where Jane lay. Coming from Jane.

I was with her, my hand on her heart faster than the great Salvator reached the finish line on his best day.

The beat was slow and it was faint, but it was there. I was on the room phone and calling an old friend I'd known was here in Saratoga, the track vet. I dialed without even knowing I knew his number. It was just there, in my head, as perfect as a petunia.

"Hank. Don't ask. Don't argue. Don't say no. Be here before I hang up. Bring everything you'd need for the worst. No. Not me and not sick. Cut up. Bad. And bring blood."

His voice was tinny over the hotel line. "What kind of blood?"

"Dog blood."

"I work on horses. Not dogs."

"Sure. But sometimes one of the horses has a dog. And it needs blood."

"True. So where are you?"

"The pink joint on Case Street. Right, that one—the Pascal House."

I'd known Hank Hanson since he was a newsie with a spot by "Patience," the south side lion on the steps of the New York City Public Library. How he got to be a vet beat me (it's so easy to lose track of people), but I always knew that like me, he was one for the ponies. His way turned out a little different than Paul's or mine. If I said that again, I'd exchange the word "little" for the words "a lot." His way was a lot different.

Hank looked like a picture I once saw in a magazine, someone's idea of what early man might have been like.

Hank Hanson was exactly the kind of fella the military would of tried to get killed as soon as possible. But Hank, besides being as hairy as Flo's best coat, had bad eyes and flat feet. So there went his chance to meet Hitler. Or Emperor Hirohito.

Ten minutes later, when Hank slammed open the door to room number 3, he found me on the floor holding Jane. Both of us were covered in blood. A dog's blood is no different than human blood. It's red and it's wet and it's sticky. It's life. This blood was Jane's life. And it was running out.

Not a word of greeting or asking what happened, Hank knelt down, adjusted his glasses, lenses like the bottom of a bottle of Dr. Pepper, and went to work, muttering. "Nine, ten, eleven wounds. A knife. What the fucking hell? Why? A dog? Comes in here and stabs a dog to death? Sonofabitch could of shot her. But too much noise. That's why. Too much noise. But look at this place. Look at this place. She fought and that must have made one hell of a racket. Oh hell, this one is deep."

I heard all this. I understood it. I didn't care. Not then. But I finally caught his eye and when I did I hated what I saw. There was no hope in it. Not even a hope of a hope.

"But she's not dead, Hank."

"She will be. And soon."

"You can't do a thing?"

"Sure. I can patch her up. But I don't give her the chance whoever did this gave her."

"Try!"

"Oh, I'll try. I always try. That's what I do. But there's no time to take her anywhere. Clear off that desktop and do it now. You're my nurse."

I was up and shoving things off the hotel's dainty desk before he finished telling me to. Smashed a pink glass ashtray on the floor, lost the writing paper and the ink pen between the wall and the desk. Hank had Jane lying on it a second later. While he hooked up a drip feed, I pressed my hand over the deepest cut.

"Keep the pressure on until I tell you to stop."

"You bet."

And so Hank Hanson began the hopeless task of saving Babe Duffy's dog. Only she wasn't Babe Duffy's dog anymore; she was mine.

Someone killed my dog. Which meant someone knew she knew them. They knew, alive, she would find them. Which meant I was close.

At that moment, I didn't care. All I could think of was my singing dog dying on the top of a flimsy decorative desk in a pink hotel that told her through me, and in the nicest possible way: "Keep Out."

31

I was standing over Hank, asking him the kind of stupid questions anxious people ask, sweating through my shirt but not smoking or drinking as I watched him work on the worst of the stab wounds.

"You think he came for her, not for me?"

"Who's he?"

"The jockey killer."

"You know who did it?"

"No. But I think Jane did."

"You've answered your own question. Could you shut up? I need to concentrate."

Hank was right. I needed to shut up. I was right too. Someone came to kill Jane. Hank was also right about a gun; guns make the sort of noise people notice. But he didn't bring a knife. The steak knife I'd found in Jane was already here, in a drawer, provided by my pink hotel. What was the plan here? Choke her? Poison her? Whatever it was, he didn't know who he was dealing with. That explained why so many wounds.

Hank said, "For pete's sake, Russo, go do some detecting. Knock on the other doors, find out if someone saw something."

Good thinking. I was a detective. Time to detect. And then the room phone rang.

Scared the spinach out of me. I answered with a clipped and shaky, "What!"

It was Marshall Hutsell, the man who'd called me back on Staten Island, the man who'd hired me for whoever he hired me for. All along, I'd assumed it was the track management. Now I was sure it was the track management.

I had no time for any of 'em.

"Hang up, Hutsell. I'm busy here."

He acted like I'd just sung him *Yes, We Have No Bananas.*
"Mr. Russo. Please come to the Saratoga Jockey Club
immediately."

I winced. Not because of Hutsell. I'd caught a clear view
of Hank rearranging something inside Jane. I said, "Where
the hell is that?"

He said, "You're a detective. Find it."

Then he hung up.

"Hank, where's The Jockey Club?"

"In New York City."

"Excuse me?"

"In Saratoga, a smaller bunch meets wherever they feel
like meeting. I imagine tonight it's at the track. Get out of
the light. She's dying but I'd still like to try."

"Dying?"

"Haven't you been listening?"

"Jane isn't dying."

"Sam, you have to be all grown-up now."

"Who says? Can you do without me? I won't go if you
can't. They can fire me. Hell, they can fuck themselves."

"She can do without you. I can do without you. I've
already done most of what I can do. Now she has to do what
she's going to do."

"But she'll be all alone."

"Nah, she won't. This place is perfect. Who would think
to look for me here? And brother, do I need the rest. I'll
stay and watch her. Maybe get a little sleep. My line of
work, I'm a light sleeper."

I should of hugged him for that. I babbled my thanks
instead.

"Go. Sooner you go. Sooner you're back."

I washed my bloody body, changed my bloody clothes,
and then I was gone.

Washing, I thought of something. Mrs. Willingford was
at the Grand Union bar when Jane was attacked. Unless she
could run faster than Fleeting Fancy, not to mention, wash
and change her clothes even faster, Willingford could not
have kill... stabbed my dog.

The man behind the big leather topped desk in the high-ceilinged room where the walls were like my walls back in Room 4-A: smothered under framed photos of horses and jocks, stood to shake my hand.

His frames were gold. Mine were just frames. But the horses were the same horses.

The desk was all show and no substance—like the smile that went with the handshake. That smile must of earned some dentist somewhere enough to buy his own island.

To one side of him, a second man sat in a button-backed burgundy leather chair. He needed the chair. The chair, not used to holding up that much weight, could of done without him. He shook my hand. His hand was wet. A third man, the one lighting a Havana stogie over by the drinks display, was Marshall Hutsell. I could tell he was going to shake my hand too, but I'd had enough of hand shaking.

"Forget all the hand jobs. Why am I here?"

That made the man with the terrific choppers laugh. "Good one, good one."

That made the fat man mad. I think he expected what he said next to come out nice, but it came out in a long snaky wheezy hiss. "You're here so we can thank you in person for the great job you've done—"

"Done?"

"And to wish you every success in the future."

"You mean I really *am* fired?"

The man behind the desk wrenched the conversation back from the fat man. If I'd made the fat man angry, the fat man had made the big cheese—after all, he did occupy the bigger chair and the great big desk—angrier. "No, of course not. We're merely telling you that it's over. The deaths were accidents. Therefore your services will no longer be required. Marshall?"

Marshall, making himself what looked like a martini, turned around to face the man behind the desk. "Yeah, Harold?"

"Please get out the club checkbook."

I said, "They weren't accidents."

The fat man leaned forward as far as his stomach allowed,

which wasn't far. "My name is Richard Dickman Todd the Third. I own more horses than you'll ever manage to bet on. Would you like to make a wager on that?"

"I never bet on the chalk."

That made the dentist's best friend laugh again.

Still laughing, Harold said, "Never place a bet on the favorite, eh? You are a wise man, Mr. Russo. And a wise man knows when to bet and when to let a race go. I think this man, gentlemen, is a wise man. He deserves a bonus, don't you agree, Richard?"

"I do indeed, Harold," hissed the fat man who was the third Richard in whatever unlucky family was stuck with him. In the hog business, would be my guess. I also loved his middle name. "I've always believed in paying the help well. It makes them more—helpful."

I stood there, feeling as fizzy as the Big Red Spring that bubbled up out of the racetrack's picnic grounds, while Marshall slapped a huge leather-bound checkbook on the big leather covered desk so that Harold, whose last name had not been mentioned, could begin writing what I hoped was a nice big check made out to me. For what? I knew for what. To send me off happy. To make me quit like a good boy.

I took the check. I took it for Jane. I needed to pay Hank. I took it because now I also needed to pay my own hotel bill. But not at the little pink place. I was thinking more along the lines of some place more expensive. Somewhere closer to where Mrs. Willingford spent a lot of her time. Somewhere I could find most of the people I needed to find by merely leaning on a pillar in the lobby.

Whether these guys liked it or not, I was solving these three cases in one—for Jane. And for the kids someone killed. As for Saratoga's Jockey Club, it could go jump in Walker's lake or crash its cars in McBartle's tree or choke on Duffy's finger food for all I cared.

Before I left, I had a good look at Marshall. Not a hair out of place, not a spot of blood on his tailored jacket. But the pink hotel was no real distance from the track.

I'd spent my time talking to Clay about what could be going on while at the same time more of it was going on.

Getting fired by these guys was like getting laid off by a sweat shop. The relief felt like a bath. I felt clean again. All I cared about was getting back to that bloody room in the pink hotel ("No Dogs Allowed") to see if I still had a dog. I didn't know why. I'd never given dogs much thought, not even when I was a kid and liked Asta in *The Thin Man* movies. But Jane wasn't just a dog. She was a talking dog. I liked her. I liked her a lot.

Pocketing the check, I read the name on the brass plaque bolted to a block of teak or whatever wood was going dear this year. Harold George Whitman.

I'd heard of him. He didn't actually own Saratoga Springs, but he might as well have.

Opening my own door was hard. I was afraid. Something important was on the other side.

Fully clothed in an old long sleeved shirt and a new vet's coat, Hank was sound asleep on my bed. It didn't look like he'd merely lain down. It looked like he'd collapsed. Before that, he'd cleaned up my little kitchen, put things away, wiped up most of the blood from the floor and walls.

With him, snuggled in the crook of his arm and wrapped up like an Egyptian mummy, was Jane. Breathing.

I sat in a chair smoking one cigarette after another for hours and thought and watched a dog breathe and thought some more. Clay had left a little bourbon in my hip flask, but I ran out of that long before I figured things out.

Three, maybe three-fifteen in the morning, I shook Hank awake. He wasn't pleased until he remembered where he was and why. "Jane dead?"

"No. But someone thinks she is, wouldn't you agree?"

Hank sat up, slapping the top of my night table trying to find his glasses. "Makes sense."

I found them for him. "Here. So if that someone finds out she isn't dead, they'll try again. You agree with that too?"

By now, Hank had his glasses on and was smacking his lips. "Water. I need water."

I got him a glass of water. He'd rolled over and was

checking on Jane before he drank it, then it went down in one long gulp. "Didn't expect her to last this long. Tough little doggie."

"Did you hear what I said, Hank?"

"Sure. If Jane survives this, you want her to be dead to whoever killed her."

"Exactly. So she can't stay here and neither can I. Whoever did this, did a thorough job of it. Right now the killer's sound asleep assuming the best. But if you, an animal doc, stay here, he'll get the picture soon enough."

"So true."

"So you're both leaving."

"Where we going?"

"You're going back to work—"

"Damn."

"Jane's going with you. We'll take her out now. Like she'd died. I'll find some old box. And you'll go home where you'll hide her until she gets well."

"Ah gee, Sam. She isn't gonna— "

"I'm leaving too."

"Leaving? Where you going?"

"I am now unemployed."

"So that's why they called. You got thrown out on your ear."

"You got that right. But they gave me a nice fat bonus for nothing. Some of which is yours for Jane.

"I don't want— "

"Shaddup. And some of which is going to get me a room in the Grand Union Hotel. Two nights maybe."

"What the hell for?"

"To make a spectacle of myself."

32

I'd snuck out of hotels at five a.m. I'd never checked into one that early—and never one so grand as the Grand Union.

The desk clerk was there, just as I expected he'd be. I don't think he was supposed to be sleeping upright in his chair. I hated to wake him but I needed a room. Hitting the solid brass desk bell, the guy came awake so fast he smacked himself in the forehead with the side of his hand. Shit. He was saluting. Like me, the poor guy had seen his share of the war.

I wondered when he'd get over it. I wondered when I'd get over it. Maybe we never would.

I got a ride in elevator number 9, me cracking my jaw, I was yawning so hard. If not for Alonzo, I don't think I'd of made it to my room on the third floor. Being the season, it was about the last one they had, small and at the back. If I'd looked, I'd find a nice view of the parking lot and all those parked cars, each one a dream. Not my dream. I didn't dream about cars.

I didn't look out the window. Holding on to the wall, I asked Alonzo if he'd mention to the right people, the kind of people who would mention it to the other right people, that I was in the hotel. He said of course he would. He said it would be his great pleasure. I tipped him well. Unlike Clay, he kept it all just like the last time I'd tipped him.

I was out of my clothes, my clothes landed wherever they landed—I was asleep in seconds.

It wasn't more than a few minutes later when someone was knocking on my door.

Fucking hell, as us PIs say (but not in the books I'd read), couldn't a guy get any sleep? Especially at these prices? So I covered my head with the goose down pillow.

It didn't work. I could still hear the knocking.

I was out of the bed and across the room in one second flat. I jerked open the door all ready to yell whatever came out of my mouth.

The words died in my throat.

It was Mrs. Willingford, all smiles and moxie. Behind her, following on as she strolled into my room, was a beautifully dressed young man pushing a beautifully dressed cart covered in a beautiful breakfast. Including champagne. That guy was all smiles too. Which made me look down. I was naked as a jay bird.

"It's about time you got up," said Mrs. Willingford, first tipping, then waving away the guy who'd rolled the tray into the middle of my little room, "and I see you are too. How charming."

By then I had at least half the bedding wrapped around me. "Up? I just got down."

"But sweetie, it's eight. And we have so much to do."

I was starving. The food smelled great. And so did Mrs. Willingford. She also looked great. Dolled up like she was off to the races. It had to take hours to look like that. What the hell time did she get up?

"I hear you've solved the case. I ought to say cases." She was strolling around my room, sniffing at the décor. "Accidents, my ass. They were murders. I've heard the Grand Union had rooms like this, though I've never seen one."

"It's fine. Go away."

She glanced out my window. "Oh look. There's two of Joker's cars. And Woody!" She was waving.

"Woody?"

"My driver. He's waiting for us."

"Semaphore I'm not coming."

"Of course you're coming. But first—breakfast. You like sweet things?"

"Who doesn't?"

"Have a strawberry."

Opening my mouth for my next wisecrack, she popped a berry in. Like Babe Duffy, I almost choked.

"There's cream where that came from."

Mrs. Willingford began taking off her clothes.

She had the type of beauty Vivian Leigh had. There was a little mole on her perfect right breast, a small scar on her smooth left thigh, her knees were dimpled. She was the color of cream, as hot as a pistol, one that's seen action in one of those gunfights with Bonnie and Clyde, and as willing as her name. What's a red-blooded male supposed to do?

I fucked her.

What I thought was Joker Willingford's wife couldn't stand being rejected. It drove her nuts. If I gave her what she needed, she'd leave me alone.

Who was I fooling? I wasn't thinking at all.

Afterwards, the both of us gleaming all over with hard earned sweat, eating her breakfast, smoking the usual cigarettes, I wondered if I'd just made the worst mistake in my life as a PI?

Sam Russo had bedded a suspect. Little chance of it happening again. The rest of 'em were guys.

Mrs. Willingford crushed out her butt in the ashtray on her side of my bed, slid out from under the covers with athletic grace, used the bathroom, got dressed, touched up her hair and make-up, leaned over for a kiss goodbye, and left. All in complete silence.

Hold on. Didn't she say I was coming? And then I got it.

It took ten minutes before I noticed the piece of paper under the ashtray. I bathed and shaved before I read it. I wasn't anxious to read it. When did she have time to write it? Of course. At her toilette. It could of said anything and none of it flattering. But I had to read the damn thing sometime and sometime had to be before I left for the track. So I read it.

It said: *As I said, they weren't accidents. But no one will ever prove it. You weren't bad and I ought to know. Mrs.W.*

I must have looked at that piece of paper forever. It sure seemed like forever. Was she telling me she did it and I'd never catch her? Was she telling me she knew who did it, and I'd never catch them? I had no idea what she was telling me. I only knew what I already knew. Three jockeys were murdered and those who counted in Saratoga Springs wanted that shut up, covered over, and forgotten.

Mrs. Joker Willingford counted in Saratoga Springs. She counted wherever highbred horses were run. Was she one of those who wanted it shut up—it didn't look like it.

A man wasn't at his best just out of the sack with a beautiful woman. I mean, he might have felt his best, but his brain was off somewhere smelling roses.

Forget that. There was enough of me left to know this: I was out of a job, but not out of money. I was solving this case if it got me killed too. I swore this on the memory of my murdered mother. And on the life of Jane.

Clean and freshly shaved, I climbed back in bed, punched the pillow a few times, and fell asleep.

33

I woke up for a second time at noon. What the hell should I do now? I couldn't check on Jane. Everyone knew about Jane. We'd been all over the track. She'd even caught a scent—then lost it in a pile of horse dung. What if I was being watched? Alonzo had done his job well. How else did Mrs. Willingford find me so quickly?

Was I being watched *before* I moved into the Grand Union? Of course I was being watched. Maybe by more than the eyes in the head of down-on-his-luck George Labold. How else would whoever it was know when to attack Jane? OK. So what if that someone followed me today? I had to assume they would. For instance, today's early morning wake-up call. That could of been Mrs. Willingford's way of checking on Jane. But no Jane. So she left me a snotty self-satisfied note. If that's what it was.

I'd had moments of doubt before this, but this time I really thought I might be better off selling insurance—like Walter Huff in James M. Cain's *Double Indemnity*. Walter was doing just fine until he met Phyllis Nirdlinger and Phyllis Nirdlinger's doomed husband.

There was one strawberry left and a little champagne. I dropped the strawberry into the glass, drank the champagne, and chewed the berry. Was Mrs. Willingford my Mrs. Nirdlinger? If she was, who did she want me to kill?

I'd kill to talk to Hank on the telephone. I couldn't. Not even from my own room. Who knew who was at the switchboard listening? Bribed or coerced. So I had to leave that one to trust. Jane couldn't die. She wasn't built for it.

All I could do was keep going until I couldn't go any farther.

So that's what I did. I kept going.

It was what we did on Luzon. When the food ran out and

the ammo was running out and there were more and more
of them and less and less of us. When we and our mounts
were strafed from the air and missiles whistled in from the
sea. When tanks ran down rank upon rank of us. When
blood and fire and unbearable noise were our lot without
cease. When most of us, starving, ate our horses, the horses
who'd charged tanks when we asked them to, who'd taken
us places our own artillery could never go, horses who never
complained and never said no.

Growing up in the Little Kid's Lock-up never taught
me to care for my fellow man. But the horses we rode in
the Philippines, they gave me a strong and lasting love for
other kinds of life, just as valuable as ours, more loyal, more
beautiful by far, without greed, without envy, and without
murder in their hearts.

Except for maybe some cats I'd met, and Jane.

I rode a Morgan mare called Magpie. Magpie was shot
out from under me. I sat with her as she died, the ground
pocked with the craters of past explosions and soon to be
cratered with more, her lovely head in my lap. We talked.
Me in my tongue, she in hers. Magpie wasn't afraid, I could
tell from the soft look in her eye. But I was. I was afraid
because I was still alive and the world around me was still
there, beyond any hell I'd ever imagined back when Jesus
was Alan Ladd and his greatest apostle was Mister.

Hell. I'd gone and gotten all sappy. It was time to stand
up and keep going.

First thing I did was what Hank Hanson suggested I do.
Go back to the pink hotel, knock on every door, ask if anyone
had seen anyone or anything around the time I was talking to
Clay in the gents at my new hotel, the Grand Union. I got
a few slammed doors, but I also got a few answers—even if
they were all different answers. A small man in a big car had
been parked outside for over an hour doing what seemed
essentially nothing (listening to Walter Winchell was my
guess), a big man on foot walked by (the old lady who told
me said she didn't like someone on foot around after dark;
it just wasn't "nice"), a tall woman under a huge hat arrived,
spoke with the desk clerk, then left, a delivery boy knocking

on the wrong door, a kid running down a corridor—but not my corridor.

I asked the lady who mentioned the big man on foot if she noticed his shoes. She said, "Shoes, sonny? It was dark. Besides, unless they're mine and they're killin' me, I don't give a fig about shoes. All I know is he had some on. I think I woulda noticed if he didn't."

I asked the desk clerk, who had been on duty at the right time on the right night, about the tall lady in the big hat. He said, "What tall lady in a big hat? Some of the people who stay here are all wet, you ask me."

So there I was. No tall lady, or so the clerk said. A big man who could of fit the bill as the guy in the elevator with Manny Walker. It depended on how big. But no way to know if he was, or wasn't, that guy, since no one else but one nervous nellie still in her nightie and curlers saw him, coming or going—but what about a delivery boy knocking on the wrong door?

I went back for a second crack at the couple who'd been behind the "wrong door." They weren't pleased to see me the first time; the second time was even chillier. But they didn't tell me to make tracks.

They said he wasn't exactly a boy, more like maybe pushing middle age. Since they themselves were just out of diapers and freshly married, "middle age" could mean thirty. They said he wore what a delivery boy should be wearing, a dark blue delivery uniform but neither could recall if there was an insignia over his pocket. And if there was, what it was. They said with a bright light over their door, and him being right under it, his face was in shadow and difficult to see. They said that he said he was sorry once and once only. I asked if he'd asked where the right room was. They said, nope, he'd just said sorry and was on his way while they got back to handicapping the next day's races—or whatever they were doing. I asked for a physical description. One said he wasn't all that big. The other said he wasn't all that small either. To both, he seemed to be maybe sort of tall.

"Really tall?"

"Well," said the male half of the reluctant duo, "maybe

not really tall. Hell, how would I know? I'm pretty tall myself if you haven't noticed."

I got in one more question before they shut the door in my face. What was he delivering? Didn't know, he didn't say, snapped the tall man who was about as tall as Edward G. Robinson on one of his tall days. But they didn't notice him carrying anything.

I said thank you to a closed door.

It was the delivery "boy." I was sure of it. With Lino, I would get these kinds of hunches. Lino always thought each one was like some sort of miracle. But then, Lino himself was the real miracle. I mean, dumb as a rock, yet he kept his job. But a hunch wasn't some kind of mysterious knowing without knowing. A hunch was just plain knowing because all sorts of little things added up. Like wearing a delivery uniform a guy could get rid of quick if it got bloody, and still walk up and down nice suburban streets without scaring old ladies.

Things were adding up. I wasn't ready to sit around and write it all down yet, make a few lists, but I was getting there. First, I had to go create a big splash at the track. I had to stroll through the upper tiers where the bigwigs hung out. I had to wander through the jockeys' dressing room. I had to hang out at the paddock watching the horses parade before their races. If whoever tried to kill Jane (she *was* alive, I knew that because I needed to know it) thought he'd succeeded—and why not? he'd tried hard enough—then he probably figured he was safe. I'd also bet a wad on everyone who counted in the Saratoga racing game knowing I'd been booted out of the picture. Even Mrs. Willingford could be thinking I was on my way home with my tail between my legs.

But I thought if I showed up at the track, doing what I'd been doing all along, things ought to shake out a little. That's what I needed right now. To shake things up.

Especially as this day was the day before the 79th running of the Travers Stakes—the first was held in 1864 but a few got missed along the way. The Travers was the best Saratoga had to offer. It was the race Fleeting Fancy was running in.

The Willingford's filly had one real competitor: Ace Admiral. Ace Admiral was a great horse. His trouble was that last year and this year Calumet Farm's Citation was winning everything. And what he wasn't winning, his stablemate, Coaltown, was winning.

The owners of Ace Admiral were carefully choosing their spots. They'd entered him in the Travers because Coaltown wasn't entered in the Travers, and neither was Citation. They hired the best jockey they could get: Ted Atkinson, twice the leading jockey in North America.

Their only real competition? Fleeting Fancy under a green and eager kid called Toby Tyrrell.

34

An hour of working the track and I was pleased with myself. I got stared at, whispered about, and ignored. All this happened in all the right places by all the right people.

Mrs. Willingford, for once standing around with Joker Willingford, didn't turn away when I walked by. But she looked right through me. At the same time, with the skill of a pickpocket—pretended to bump into me: oh, I *am* sorry—slipped another note in my jacket pocket. I probably knew what it said, but people can surprise you.

I'd save it for a quiet moment.

At the track, when the horses were running, there were no quiet moments. Or quiet places to read private notes—not unless I wanted to be seen and make it part of my "act."

I didn't. Who knew what that rich and crazed skirt had written?

The only two people who spoke to me were the exact two I expected to speak to me. Saratoga's shining example of wit and honesty, that great security guard Carroll Goose, and a keyed-up Paul Jarrett. Paul was back in the purple number with those grotesque yellow flowers. As for Goose, he was actually manning his post by the betting windows. Since he considered himself "working," all I got was a slap on the back and a grin, which was all I could stand. He'd been drinking. What a surprise. Paul, on the other hand, was pacing the hall outside the jock's room. Getting threatened by three goons didn't seem to of rustled a feather, but as an agent, waiting around for the results of each race was making him sweat. His cut of every dollar they won was one dollar farther away from getting hit over the head with a baseball bat. Or shot in the back. Or even the stomach. Whichever way, it was bound to hurt.

A goon with a gat is usually a goon who itches to use

it. There aren't that many classy mopes out there. Just one
more thing I was learning about being a PI. Bogie was always
talking to some colorful cheeseball with a great barber, an
even better tailor, and a terrific vocabulary. I was beginning
to get it. Bogie was in the movies and somebody in a place
called Hollywood was writing those lines he spoke and the
lines spoken to him.

It was no fun growing up. Your dreams got more and
more about what you *felt* like, plus this and that damn personal
thing, and less and less about what you *wanted*, like pirates
and cowboys and PIs with a way with words and dames.

Turning at the end of the hall so he could pace on back,
Paul jumped a little when he saw me. He also didn't look
too good. Like maybe he'd caught something. I hoped it
wasn't catching. I made the worst patient, especially since
there was never any nurse but me. Most of all, I hoped it
wasn't what Labold caught. And then I caught myself. Paul,
snitch for fat cats? That'd be the day.

"Jeez, Russo. Don't sneak around like that."

"I'm not sneaking around. I'm doing my best to be
seen."

"Why? I heard you solved the case. You almost had me
convinced, but they turned out accidents after all."

"Who told you that?"

"Everybody." He was patting his pockets, all of them,
one after the other. I took pity and gave him a cigarette—
which reminded me I had an unread note in my pocket. That
distracted me for about a second. I really would save it for
when there was a moment where I wasn't "on show."

Paul, inhaling half the smoke in one drag, said: "So where
you going now?"

"I'm not going anywhere. None of the cases are solved
and until they are, I'm not leaving."

Paul laughed, a real laugh from deep in his belly. "Ain't
that just like you. I should of known."

"If you were me, Paul, would you walk away?"

"If I was you? Never. But since I'm me, yep, I'd walk.
Job's not paying so what's the point?"

"The point is I took the job in the first place and pay or

no pay, it isn't over."

Paul slapped me on the shoulder. The slightest yelp from my kidney reminded me of one of my many adventures in Saratoga Springs. "That's my Sam. A brave heart through and through. And stubborn as hell."

I said, "How's the races coming? You collecting winners?"

He shrugged. "Mostly shows and places. But it's still money and I got faith."

"That's my Paul."

I left him there to pace and went on down to the paddock. The paddock at any track has to be about my favorite place. Horses ready to run are parading by, nostrils flared, hides jumping, some sweating, some plodding, some with hooves dancing. The jocks in their silks are taking last minute instruction from trainers or enduring an owner's opinion.

The smell of leather and horse and hope. I loved it.

Toby Tyrrell was already up on number nine, a big rangy bay who looked like he was sleepwalking. A lot of guys don't bet a horse like that. They figure he'd sleep in the paddock, he'd sleep in the race. But a horse like that is relaxed. Why work up a sweat before you have to? I liked the look of the nag. I checked my sheet. Horse's name was New World, a son of Geisha by Discovery. Discovery was producing some great broodmares. Who knew? Geisha could be one of them. New World hadn't yet shown much in three starts, but he was improving. It said so, right in the paper.

I was supposed to be showing my face. Showing it at a betting window seemed as good a place as any.

As I was turning toward the closest window, I caught Toby's eye. He'd been adjusting one of New World's stirrups. Straightening up, he saw me. How could he miss seeing me? I was less than five feet away, on the other side of the barrier. We stared at each other for what felt like time enough to grow beards. I did it well. Practice makes perfect, they say—and I'd been doing a lot of staring since I decided I was Bogart.

Toby lost his race by a nose. One more furlong, it would of been his and New World's by three lengths.

Dropping down from the saddle, he saw me again, blinked, turned an interesting shade of red right up to his hairline, then did something I tried to follow. His eyes, frightened, were looking for something, or more like someone, behind me. I turned—but whoever it was, wasn't there. Or had already turned away.

If he'd been reacting to someone, the choice of who it could be included everyone I knew here or who knew me. They were all at the paddock looking over the entries for the 4th at Saratoga.

The members of the Jockey Club, including Marshall Hutsell and the other two puffed up swells, milled about. They'd paid me off and kissed me off. It was swell watching their faces once they caught a load of me: surprised, displeased, disturbed.

Mr. and Mrs. Joker Willingford were not milling. Mrs. was holding up Mr. backed by a couple of flunkies in case Mrs. tripped. There was Hank Hanson. Hank wasn't there for Joker. Hank was there because he was always there, especially when the horses were running. It was his job to clean up any sad messes. I knew he was praying there wouldn't be any, just as I was.

Like me, Hank was a true blue horse lover.

And oh yeah, there was Hollie Hughes dressed as usual, like he belonged in a circus. A few jocks were lounging around, pretending they were OK not having a mount in this race—among them, Mash Mooney who'd ridden in the third, coming home fourth. Mash was listening to his agent, George Labold. George had a grip on Mash like they were both drowning. Probably because of Mash losing. The Travers was coming up fast. Labold was furious. Mash was taking it like he had it coming.

Over by the path that led from the paddock to the track was Carl Hessing, the claiming trainer who'd rented me a dashing steed, the one I rode to see how long it would take to get to the lake Manny Walker drowned in. Carl was chewing on a stogie. Probably had a horse in something; probably praying no one would claim it.

Behind them all, keeping a safe respectful distance from

the "white folk" in an area "reserved" for blacks, was Thomas Clay Jefferson. And why not? Even Clay got a day off now and then. Clay, somehow smaller without his Grand Union uniform, was surrounded by what I assumed was family.

I tried catching his good eye. He was too busy looking over a form sheet with a fellow who looked like his father.

Pacing back and forth near a beer stand was Paul Jarrett. I had to hand it to Paul. He was game. Any minute the people he owed could walk him away, tired of waiting for their money. But here he was, just like me, making a show of it.

The biggest stand-out was Mrs. Willingford. Taken up with my own business, I only now noticed today's hat. It was black, small and feathered. On someone else's head it'd look like a dead crow. On hers, it looked smart. The dress was black and so were her shoes. But most funereal of all was the flower she held. A black tulip.

At least it wasn't a black dahlia. Police out in L.A. were getting nowhere with that one. A girl in a vacant lot, sawed in half at the waist, her mouth sliced open from each painted corner all the way up to each delicate ear. Bad. Really bad.

Pamela Teager was worse than that. Because of her age and because of her child and because of the sawing. I wish I'd never seen it. Glad I'd never see the girl they called "The Black Dahlia."

I figured I'd made my play. By now, everyone who needed a good look at me, had gotten their look. No one was looking now. It was Mrs. Willingford who had most of them wondering, and those who weren't wondering about her and her black tulip, were wondering about their bets.

Stepping behind a hawker of hotdogs and bottled beer, it was time to read the note she'd slipped in my pocket.

It said: *You owe me. I'd like paying please. Tonight.*

35

I wasn't trying to make heads or tails of who killed Walker, McBartle and Duffy. I wasn't sneaking over to Hank's to know the truth about Jane—if she was alive, I'd get her killed; if she was dead, it would ruin my day and night and probably mess with a lot more of my time. I wasn't worrying about Mrs. Willingford's note—"Tonight" was still long enough away I could pretend it might never come. What I was doing was lying on my bed in one of the smallest rooms offered by the Grand Union Hotel remembering a time back at the Staten Island Home for Children. I knew exactly what year it was. A horse bred in Kansas took the Kentucky Derby.

By the finish line, Lawrin, bred for sprinting, was dropping from pure exhaustion, but he kept on running. I never forgot that. Lawrin kept on running—just like I was doing.

In Lawrin's year I was doing what I usually did in the evening, hanging around outside the window of Mister's private shack listening to whatever he was listening to on the radio. Lino was on one side of me, chewing gum. Lino always chewed gum if he could get it; if he couldn't get fresh he had a stash of abc stuck under his bed. Paul was on the other side of me, leaning in so hard one more push and Lino and I would of fallen over into the closest bush.

After dark, us kids were locked in for the night. All except kids like Lino and Paul and me. We were the adventurous type. Us and some others were out whenever we wanted to be by climbing down a length of homemade rope—made out of old sheets we'd found in the back of the so-called linen closet—we'd hung from a bathroom window. The window was on the third floor. We'd jimmied that one open around about the time we learned the term: to jimmy. When not in

use, we made sure "our" window was closed and that when
it was closed it looked like it could never be opened. The
"rope" we kept hidden under a special floorboard. I'd bet
it was still there. If it was, there'd also be a bunch of other
things we'd stashed away over the years.

Seeing them now, I wondered what I'd think. I probably
wouldn't think. I'd probably cry. That home was tough.

Anyway, that night the show was *Gang Busters*. Tires
squealing. Machine guns blatting. Police whistles. Over all
that racket, Mister couldn't of heard us, even if one of us had
fallen off his shack into a bass drum.

Then it was: *Brought to you by Palmolive Soap, tonight, Gang
Buster's presents*—heart stopping pause—*The Case of the Big
Switcheroo*. Or something like that. It was always something
like that. And we were glued to Mister's outside wall, rain
or snow or sleet or hail.

I used to listen to the tales of G men with my hair on
end, struggling to keep my balance between two other kids
who were as bewitched as me.

Maybe it was *Gang Busters* more than Bogie that got me
where I was today. Beaten up, fired, knowing for sure I had
a case (three cases) but not close to solving them, my dog
stabbed, and sure to be getting a visit from Mrs. Willingford
before the night was out.

I watched the fan on the Grand Union ceiling. Three
fat blades moving round and round and round, pushing the
sluggish Saratoga air—air smelling of sulfur. Getting sleepy.
Getting sleep—what was I thinking? Something about
Gang Busters. Only a minute ago, two minutes ago—what
was it? Oh right, I remember. Listening to Mister's radio.
Palmolive Soap. Machine guns ratt-attat-ting. But there was
never a *Case of the Big Switcheroo*. That was just something
that popped into my head.

Switcheroo.

Like the shell game played on a sidewalk in any big city
from sea to shining sea, the game any carny worth a single
red cent got suckers to play. It was a mug's game. Three
cups on a board and under one of the cups, a dried pea. But
the pea was palmed. It was never under a cup. Three jockeys

on a racetrack and under one of the jocks, a fast horse. But the riders were dead. None of them rode the horse.

I got it. I understood.

How do you compare human evil? Was Hitler worse than Stalin? Did Albert Fish beat Mister in the Bad Guy Stakes? Was bumping off talented young jocks as bad as bumping off innocent kids?

I'd fallen asleep dreaming of shell games and *Gang Busters* when my door opened up and in walked Joker Willingford's wife. I'd locked the door. But that was nothing to someone like her. She simply bribed one of the staff to open it.

This time I was fully clothed, confused by being suddenly woken up, and one eye was glued shut with sleep.

"You look dazzling, honey pie," said Mrs. Willingford, sweeping across the room and coming to a perfect landing on the edge of my bed.

I would of said thank you, but my mouth wasn't working yet. I hate naps. I especially hate naps when someone slams you out of one.

When I could think, what I thought was Mrs. Willingford was going to take off her clothes again, an act bound to wake me up, but she surprised me—as usual.

First surprise was her clothes. She was wearing a man's dark shirt, a pair of men's slacks, and a man's hat. She looked great.

"What happened to the tulip?"

"I ate it."

"I believe you."

The second surprise was when she pinched me.

"Ouch!"

"We have things to do," she said, "so get up, wash your face and open that eye. It's creepy. Then let's go."

"Things to do?"

"You bet. Didn't you get my note?"

"Sure I did. Both of 'em."

"Then why act dumb?"

"I'm acting dumb?"

"Dumber than Joker. Of course, Joker has an excuse.

He's older than—who's that really old guy in the Bible?"

"Methuselah."

"Yeah, him. Come on, before it's too late."

"Where are we going?"

"Where you should have been going ever since you proved those poor kids weren't murdered."

"Why do you think I proved—where's that?"

"Confronting the killer."

"What?"

"Oh shut up and come on. I told you they weren't accidents. You know they weren't accidents. Even though everyone and their Auntie Sue wants 'em to be accidents. S'why I wore black today. Mourning." By now I was on my feet with my face in a bowl full of cold water. But I could still hear well enough. "I'll be damned if someone gets to bump off jockeys around me. I know you've made assumptions about me—why wouldn't you? Just as I've made assumptions about you. I married for money, you bet I did. Any woman with an ounce of brains would. But I married money that included horses. You like horses?"

"More than— "

"People. Same here. So I've been paying attention. Done some sleuthing on my own. Got my own ideas. You want to know what my assumptions are about you?"

I wasn't sure I did. But I couldn't stop myself saying, "Shoot."

"You're a greenhorn, but you're game. You aren't stupid, but you talk too much and you miss things. You talk too much and you miss things because your heart's too soft. You're in this PI game a little longer and you'll toughen up. Or maybe you're not that soft but something's happened to make you soft for now, which means it'll pass."

Damn. She was good. Better than the crone who used to read palms anywhere she could in the St. George Ferry Terminal, luring passengers coming and going to Manhattan. "Only a penny, madam, only a penny to know whatcha know you wanna know."

Mrs. Willingford was still flapping her lips. "That's good and that's bad. But no time to discuss it now. I've been waiting for you to catch up. And you would have. But we don't have any more time for you to do it on your own dime. So here I am."

By now we were out the door and into an elevator. I said, "You telling me you've come to—?"

"Help you catch up. I'm telling you I have a good idea. You figured out how it was done, and bully for you, but you still don't know why."

"I wouldn't say that. But okay. You tell me why."

"To get the ride on Fleeting Fancy."

"Hold on, sister. I already figured that was exactly why they were—"

We were out back where she kept her snazzy car. "It's worse than that."

"Worse than killing three kids?"

"Tomorrow's the Travers. Tonight, I think a horse is going down. And I won't have it."

36

Ace Admiral, whose grandpappy was the tremendous Man o' War, was a fine chestnut colt who'd had the sad misfortune of being born in the same year as Calumet Farm's Citation and Citation's stablemate Coaltown.

Being born in the same year as Citation was also the colt Coaltown's misfortune.

Ace Admiral's trainer was Jimmy Smith, son of the one and only Tom Smith who'd conditioned Seabiscuit—and you'd win big if you bet I was impressed by both father and son. Once and once only this thought crossed my mind: if only Jimmy Smith was a suspect we'd talk, about jockeys, about horses, about his dad. Too bad for me and good for him, he wasn't. For one thing, he wasn't in town when all this happened; he was down in Lexington, Kentucky, at Maine Chance Farm, training the make-up dame's horses. Elizabeth Arden, that was her name. She'd made an incredible amount of dough off every woman's worry over her looks and her fear of aging. Arden threw a lot of that dough into horse racing. So god bless Lizzie. Anyway, Jimmy, as well as Arden, saw the problem with Citation right off the bat— only two years old he'd run nine times and won eight of his starts, breaking records and other horse's hearts. Now, at three, he'd already won the Triple Crown of American horse racing and I'd make bet he wasn't anywhere near finished.

Jimmy didn't run Lizzie's damn fine horse in the Kentucky Derby or the Preakness Stakes—or even the Belmont Stakes, just in case Citation was tired. Citation wasn't tired. He tied the Belmont Stakes record set by Count Fleet.

But whenever a good race came along where Citation or Coaltown were busy racing somewhere else, Ace Admiral ran in it.

He'd just come off a win in the same race Man o' War had

also won in the year of my "birth": the Lawrence Realization Stakes over at Belmont Park. So now he was here, along with Jimmy, both in the flesh at Saratoga Springs, going for the track's most prestigious event, the Travers Stakes. He was also favored to win it, although the betting was heavy on the Willingford filly Fleeting Fancy.

This was important stuff, what I was thinking. Ace Admiral was the horse Mrs. Willingford was sure was going down.

Mrs. W'd parked her car behind a classy restaurant on Union Avenue—the place was jumping with people already celebrating the Travers—tossed the keys to the gimpy attendant who obviously knew her well, told him to watch both keys and car, and then we walked. In the dark. Together. Straight up Union Avenue towards the track. Which was closed this time of night. Except, of course, to people like Mrs. Willingford. Aside from any other reason, she had horses stabled there. As for me, I may not of been banned, but I sure wasn't welcome.

Creeping along, I told her I'd have to sneak in. She told me that suited her fine since *she* was sneaking in. Why else leave her car blocks away, hidden among a hundred other cars behind a restaurant? Why else wear her sneaking-around-in-the-dark clothes?

I said, "Oh."

My clothes weren't as sneaky as hers because I didn't have any sneaking-around stuff. I was a PI. I should of had clothes like that. Note to Sam Russo: if you ever get another job as a sleuth, find the best sneaky clothes money can buy. Especially the shoes. Mine were squeaking with every other step.

For this, I was told to stop and take them off.

"But there's rocks and stickers."

"Knock it off, Mr. Whiny. Those shoes'll wake the horses if they don't wake everything else. Cripes. I should be the PI here."

Untying my shoes as I sat on a bale of hay, then stuffing one in my right jacket pocket and the other in my left jacket pocket, I had to agree with her. But I didn't have to tell her

I agreed with her.

Her plan, which I was expecting to hear the details of any minute—although, not being entirely a fool as well as a person who was well read in these matters—I was fairly sure I knew the basics.

We were sneaking in to stop foul play. Someone had killed three jockeys. One of those dead jockeys was set to ride Fleeting Fancy. The other two were on lesser horses. With Fancy's rider dead, some jock could of ditched his own ride and made a grab for Fancy's empty saddle. With all three dead, his chances of getting it was pretty good. Until Toby picked up the mount. But Toby wasn't seasoned. He could make a mistake.

He could also be the killer.

Whoever did this would need Fancy to win. Killing three jockeys and having her lose was a waste of three dead jockeys. But Ace Admiral was running and Ace was the favorite. And rightly so. Ace Admiral'd just done his grandpappy proud in the Lawrence Realization Stakes. For icing, Ted Atkinson was riding him and Ted Atkinson was North America's leading jockey in both 1944 and 1946. Even worse for Fleeting Fancy, he was the first jockey to win more than a million bucks in one season.

Fancy could beat Ace. I knew that the first time I saw her. I also knew—who in the game didn't?—any horse could be beaten on any given day. In his entire career, Man o' War never lost a single race, except one. That was to a horse called Upset right here at this exact track. Citation lost to a nag called Saggy. Boston, vicious to the end, lost a couple, his great son Lexington lost one, and one of my favorite horses of all time, a seventeen-hand beauty called Longfellow, lost a couple more.

I loved Longfellow for more than being a horse; he was also part of one of the 19th century's most gruesome and cruel multiple murder mysteries. Two old folks, brother Jacob Harper and sister Betsey Harper, were hacked to death with a hatchet. On the same night, there was an attempt on a third brother, John Harper. Jacob and Betsey were at home. John was miles away in a barn at the Old Kentucky

Association track in Lexington.

Longfellow's owner, John Harper, was in the barn instead
of his bed at home, because he was watching over his beloved
racehorse. Back then, people did more than dope a rival
horse.

Jacob and Betsey died because they were sound asleep
in their beds. John survived because he was wide awake
with Longfellow and he wouldn't open the barn door when
someone outside called to him.

The surviving brother, John Harper, was a stinking
rich man. If he'd died alone, then his horse breeding farm,
Nantura, and all else he owned would of gone to Betsy and
Jacob. But if they all three died—well, that was the idea.

When it was over, with nothing proved, the old man
lived the rest of his life never breathing a word against his
remaining kin. But when the rich old man died in his bed,
older and richer and wiser, his will was read to an assembled
crowd of eager relatives. They discovered he'd left money
to each and every one of 'em, and to some of his "darkies."
But to two excited souls, a certain nephew and the nephew's
son—both hard up for cash and both ne'er-do-wells—not
a penny.

The Harper case preceded Lizzie Borden and her furious
ax by 21 years.

Horrible thought: if they'd succeeded in killing John
Harper, two drunken killers would of owned Longfellow.

Anyway, that's what Mrs. Willingford meant when she
said a horse was going down. If someone could kill three
young jocks and a dog, what would stop them from killing
Ace Admiral? Or at least incapacitating him? And then
watch Fancy come home first.

We dashed across East Avenue, first making sure no one
was coming either way, then worked our way through the
bushes between the road and the first of the barns. Muffling
my eeks of pain when I stepped on whatever, I was figuring
it out. I was figuring it all out. I was slow, maybe, but I
was steady. I was sentimental, maybe, but I could look
truth square in the eye. It was something you learned in a
place like the Staten Island Caged Kids Home. We grew up

barely able to read, but we knew evil when we let ourselves look. Everyone looked at Mister, but no one wanted to see him, too scary when you're too young to do much. Us not looking is how he got away for so long with what his god told him to do. Growing up in that Dickensian pile with Mister and Flo did things to a kid, some good, some bad, some a little of each.

Whoever we were supposed to be when we arrived, most as innocent as babes if not actual babes, none of us turned out that way by the time we left.

There were some early years with moments of sun and moments of laughter and moments of love for my fellow kid. But as time passed, the sun went away and the laughter got bitter and the love faded like the old clothes we wore.

When we reached the barns, I had it straight in my head. I knew who and I knew why and I knew I didn't have a shred of evidence. I knew I would of, but Jane was probably dead. I had to accept that. I couldn't keep pretending she'd survive an attack like the one I'd arrived too late to stop. I also knew I didn't give an almighty shit about evidence. I wasn't Lino. I wasn't a cop. I didn't have to do anything "by the book." Or appear to be doing it, like Lino and most of his cronies did.

Me and Mrs. Willingford weren't on our way to make an arrest. We were on our way to save a life.

37

"Be quiet. He's stabled at the end of this row."

"Where's the lights? Shouldn't there be lights? Shouldn't they be lit all night?"

"There should be," she said, "but there aren't. Not good, wouldn't you say? Not only should there be lights, grooms should be around somewhere."

"It's late. They could be sleeping in the straw."

"Could be. Better be."

It was at that point I realized that not only Ace Admiral could be in for it, but so might some poor old faithful groom. A relative of Thomas Clay Jefferson's even, or a kid like I used to be, eager to do anything to be around the horses. From where I'd been before, which wasn't happy, now I was getting mad.

Mrs. Willingford pulled her hat down lower on her head and began creeping along the shed row. Me too. I was doing the same thing, but by this time I'd taken the lead. Mrs. Willingford might be as smart as Eleanor Roosevelt and as slick as Mary Astor, but she still wasn't as strong as me, and if she had a gun, I hadn't seen it.

I suddenly stopped moving and turned. Mrs. Willingford walked right into me with a soft whoof. I asked: "You packing?"

"Am I what?"

"Carrying a gun."

"No. But I do have a sap."

"What the hell are— "

"Don't ask. Keep moving. And don't stop sudden like that again. Shssssh, my lovely."

That last was addressed to a horse who'd stuck a curious black nose over its stall door.

Aside from any noise we were making, and we weren't

making any once we'd both shut up, the night was as silent
as a night of sleeping horses. Small contented nickers, the
rustle of hay, a cat sneezing, a snoring groom or two. Even
so, there should of been a light somewhere. Which could
mean, since people were paid to make sure things worked,
someone'd turned off whatever ought to be dimly shining
down on this particular shed row.

I heard something—the sound of a stall door opening.
Could be anyone. Could be nothing. I took my gun out of
my pocket. I pointed it in the right direction. I watched a
booted foot step out from a stall, followed by the rest of the
leg, and then the man who owned both. His head looked
first one way. It looked the other. Neither the man nor his
head were large. He wasn't tall either.

What he was, was furtive.

The first way he looked didn't bother him. All he saw
was a nice long dark and empty shed row. He didn't seem to
be leaving; he seemed to be having a look around before he
did whatever he was there to do.

But looking the other way included me and Mrs.
Willingford who'd made it halfway down the row and were
still coming. I had a gun out and was pointing it right at
him.

We all stopped in the dark. Him, me, her. For what
seemed like ages, we all stayed right where we were. Then
I woke up.

"You!" I yelled, "Get away from that horse!"

At that point, a lot more than two things happened.
First, the guy bolted. The other way. Second, I bolted after
him. Third, Mrs. Willingford ran straight down the shed row
and into the stall the guy had just run out of. And lastly, and
by no means least, everything woke up at once and began
making one holy hell of a racket. Cats, dogs, goats, horses,
chickens, roosters, pigs.

The guy was fast. He was really fast. But I wasn't all that
bad myself. Hadn't completely gone to seed since the last
time I found myself running. Back then I was running away
from a whole platoon of little people who wanted to kill me
in the worst way, but I could be just as fast running towards

something. And I was catching up fast, catching up enough to grab hold of him. Problem was my shoes. They weren't on my feet, they were in my pockets. At least one was. The other had already fallen out. I'd heard it go. Running barefoot on hard ground where any number of things could be lying around slowed me down just enough so when my bare foot came down on a pointed bit of metal, I went down too.

He was sprinting away.

There was no way I was just going to shoot the guy. I hadn't seen his face. I didn't know what he'd left behind where Ace Admiral bedded down. Who knows? I could be shooting his trainer or… hell, I just couldn't shoot him.

So I lost him.

Found my shoe on the way back to Ace Admiral and Mrs. Willingford. By the time I got there, I was limping.

She was standing by Ace who was also standing. He looked fine. Arching his neck and nudging Mrs. Willingford for candy. She looked fine. Arching her own neck as she ran her hands over his body looking for anything wrong. At least from what I could see of them in the dark. What didn't look fine was the groom. He looked like he'd been hit and hit hard.

"I'll watch the horse," she said, "go get a doctor for this poor man. He get away?"

I was putting on my shoes as fast as I could. "He got away. He had shoes. How's the horse?"

"I think we got here just in time. Just like I thought, the sonofabitch was just about to drug him. Look."

She held out a syringe full of what was probably a narcotic of some sort. "Found it on the shelf over there, all ready to go. Poor horse would have lost by a mile."

"And your horse would of won."

"Probably by daylight."

The groom was coming round. Time for me to fetch a doc.

"See if he can talk," I said. "If he can, ask what happened. Get every detail."

All I got for that was a slap on the arm. "And you thought

if you didn't tell me that, I would what?"

"Forget it. I'll be back faster than Fancy."

And I would be. The closest doc, even if he was a vet, was Hank. I had to go to Hank's. I couldn't avoid it.

The guy I'd chased wasn't the big man Alonzo had seen. He wasn't the killer. I knew who he was by smell alone. Old Crow wasn't hard to mistake.

OK, so I knew who I'd run after—which was a nice little piece to fit together with all the others—but what was running off to Hank going to look like to the man who'd hired Carroll Goose to dope a horse? That man was watching from somewhere nearby. He had to be. He'd be a fool not to. He knew how things were going.

Would it cross his mind Jane wasn't dead, that she was alive at Hank's clinic? I had to trust it wouldn't. Jane was dead. A groom was hurt. What else would I do but run for the nearest medical help?

Sure I was watched every step of the way, I thought fast. The big man had just made his first big mistake. Hiring help was never a good idea when you were killing people. Or horses. Hiring Carroll Goose was his worst choice; Goose wasn't one to keep his mouth shut. He may not know the fella who'd hired him to get at Ace Admiral was the same fella who'd killed three young jockeys, but he knew what he knew.

Carroll was a dead goose by morning.

Worse than that thought was this one: I'd done all I could not to worry about Jane. It hadn't worked. I worried about Jane. Right now Jane was all I was worried about. Fuck Carroll Goose. Fuck who hired Carroll Goose. Fuck who killed three jocks. Fuck why they'd done it. For the mount? For the money they make betting on Fancy? For the sick thrill of it? Mrs. Willingford thought she knew. She was just waiting for me to catch on. I thought I knew, but it was only a thought. Jane was real. I had to know about Jane.

I had my excuse. The groom needed Hank Hanson.

Hank lived and worked in a small house on the track, not far as the crow flew. And every running step I took—painful steps, even fully shod—made my heart beat that much faster.

I couldn't hear she was dead. I wasn't built for that kind of guilt.

Hank wasn't asleep. He was working on a horse's front foot. I rushed in; he didn't even look up. "Rotation. If I get it now, I might stop it. What you want?"

"A groom. He's been sapped."

Hank gentled the horse's hoof into a bucket of slurried ice. "What? When? Where?"

"Here. Just now."

He had an assistant, a young woman built like a silo but with eyes full of life and caring. She held the horse's leg in the bucket, cooing to it all along, as Hank grabbed his bag to run after me. I was already moving fast, back towards the right shed row.

Hank caught up, running silently beside me. He did that for ten long strides before he said, "You want to ask about Jane?"

"No."

"You might as well."

"I don't want to hear."

"I would."

"I'm not you."

"She's alive, Sam. I don't know how, but she is, and she might even make it."

I would of stopped, but I couldn't. How bad was the groom hurt? How was Mrs. Willingford doing on her own? Then, a sudden gut-punch of a thought: what if the big man wasn't watching me, but instead waiting for just this thing, for me to leave so he could come back and finish the job? If he was smart—and he was smart—he'd be careful of Mrs. Willingford. But being smart, he'd figure a way.

I couldn't stop. All I could do was turn my head and gift Hank with the biggest smile I'd managed in years.

38

Mrs. Willingford was fine.

Ace Admiral was fine. Maine Chance Farm was hovering round him in force. He wouldn't be alone again until he caught his train out of Saratoga Springs, and not then either. I could of had that talk with his trainer Jimmy Smith if I'd wanted to. Hell, I *did* want to, but I had so many other things to do. Not one of 'em was talking horses.

No one would ever know it but me—but that night I had a moment to be proud of: Sam Russo acted like a PI, not a racing fan.

Ace Admiral's groom was alright, if getting smacked hard on the back of the head could be called "alright."

I've watched actors in movies get hit or socked or sapped or gut punched or shot somewhere that doesn't kill 'em. They come round pretty fast. They keep on going, maybe with a bandage or two, maybe a wince now and then, but they just keep doing whatever they were doing before they got clobbered. Out here, in real life, these things hurt. They hurt bad. No coming round fast from any of 'em. What really happens is you groan a lot, maybe throw up, maybe get dizzy and fall over—you sure wanna touch where it hurts which only makes it hurt worse. Then you get poked and prodded by a doc. If the doc thinks you ought to, a loud ambulance comes along to take you away to get your head examined.

That's what happened to the groom.

Before he was bundled off, he came round enough to answer a few questions. First the light outside went out, the dim one left on all night, every night. Then someone called his name.

I said, "Your actual name—so he knew you?"

"Well, nah. I didn't mean that. I mean someone called

out sort of quiet like. You know, inna kind of a loud whisper. He said: hey you. So I got up from where I was lying and trying to get some shuteye and went on over to the door. But nobody was there. Couldn't see anything anyway with the light gone. So I shrugged like you do when you think you been hearing things, and turned around to go back and lie down. That's when I got hit on the head."

"So you heard nothing?"

"Nope. Come to think, yes. I heard a whistley kind of noise just before I got hit. And I saw a lot of stars. So now my head feels like a cracked egg. I'm gonna be all right, right Hank?"

"You'll be fine."

OK, so where was I? The groom saw nothing. What Mrs. Willingford and I saw, we saw in the dark. But I knew who I'd chased. It wasn't who I thought I'd be chasing, but it still fit. It had to. Otherwise my whole beautiful idea fell off its horse in the last furlong. I honestly didn't think that was going to happen. The idea was too good.

I hoped.

But to be really sure, I needed my dog. I needed Jane.

I got this moment to savor what Hank said. *She's alive, Sam. I don't know how, but she is, and she'll make it.* OK, so I'd left off a few words. I had to.

When the groom was gone, and with Mrs. Willingford busy bossing the track workers into getting lights fixed faster, at the same time chewing out the night watchman for not doing his job, I took Hank aside. Figuring we were watched, I whispered: "Who knows about Jane?"

Hank, catching on, whispered back: "First me. And now you."

"What about the girl I just saw, the one working with you."

"Maisie's never seen Jane. I keep the dog in my own personal quarters."

"You don't think she's ever snuck in, had a look around?"

His "no" was emphatic, even irritated. And a little loud. But a PI's gotta ask what a PI's gotta ask.

"I was just asking."

He said, "I get it. I know as well as you do, Jane needs to be dead or he'll try again. She should be dead now. But she isn't."

"How long before she can move around?"

"Not for a long time, Sam. You want her to sniff someone, you'll have to bring that someone to her, not her to him."

"Right."

I now needed to do two things. I had to talk to Mrs. Willingford, privately. Then I had to go have a talk with a fella who was by now wondering if he should make a run for it, or just sit tight until things blew over.

First time I met Mrs. Willingford, getting her alone seemed as easy as playing chess with Lino Morelli. Now it was as hard as playing chess with Lino Morelli. Playing with Lino was painful. It hurt to sit and wait for a guy so dumb. Mrs. Willingford was as far from dumb as Lino was from smart. Tonight she was busy. Once she was sure Maine Chance wasn't taking any more chances, that every track official she could find had a piece of her mind, she was off to her own barn, me following like maybe Jane would one day follow me.

Fleeting Fancy was asleep. Her groom was asleep. All the dim lights in her shed row were on.

It was one in the morning and it was now or never.

I got in her way. It was the first time we'd made eye contact since I don't know when. "You think you know," I said, "don't you? You think you know who's doing all this. Just like you knew what had to happen tonight to make the whole nasty thing a sure bet. Or as near as."

"You bet your ass, I know. Just like I figure you know who tried to dope Ace Admiral. So go catch the bastard while I wake up the Racing Secretary and scratch Fancy."

I was ten feet away before I turned back. "Why are you scratching Fleeting Fancy?"

"I'll make you a deal."

"OK."

"You catch the killer and I'll tell you why I'm taking Fancy out of the Travers."

39

A room came with Carroll's security job, one even smaller than mine back in Stapleton. But it had a better view: the backstretch of the Saratoga racecourse.

I figured Carroll Goose was too dumb to make a run for it. He probably thought all he was doing was a job for some guy, a nasty job, true, illegal for sure, but it paid and was nothing to work up a sweat about. So it went haywire, so what? But I could of figured wrong. Goose wasn't smart, but like all men, from top to bottom, there's a built-in sense of survival, a sense that yells: hey, slub, you're in danger here.

So maybe Goose *would* make a run for it.

But first he'd go back to his room for his things. People do that, and that's where people go wrong. I'd learned that one with Lino. Police drive directly to your house or your room or your shack or your cave. They send another unit to your mother's house. Or your girlfriend's house. Or your ex-wife's. And so do the bad guys. Never go back. Cut your losses and leave.

Carroll Goose went back.

When I got there, the door to his room was closed. I expected that. But it wasn't locked. I also expected that. So I walked right in. Goose wasn't there, but he had been. Probably got there right after he lost me—which was right after I stepped on whatever I stepped on.

Goose had been there and now he wasn't. But he didn't go peaceably. I'd bet he didn't go in one piece either. His room told a story even Lino could read. No blood, so no knife. No bullet hole in a wall, no hole through the window pane, so no gun. But the guy I was hunting didn't use knives or guns. Except on dogs. He didn't make noise and he didn't make messes. Except for dogs. Unless the mess was staged

to look accidental. No time to stage whatever he'd done to
Carroll. There'd been a struggle, the couch pushed across
the room, a lamp overturned, the contents of Carroll's
hastily packed suitcase strewn over the thin carpet.

If the big man was strong enough to shove a ham
sandwich down Babe Duffy's throat and hold it there, he
was strong enough to strangle a struggling Carroll Goose.
Goose wasn't a big guy. He just had a big round face under
not much hair.

So where would the killer stash the body?

He didn't have time to get too elaborate. He didn't have
a whole lot of privacy. It was late. Pretty much all of the
other roomers were asleep. Tomorrow—or today; it was
well past midnight—was Travers Day, everyone had to be
up early and working. Carroll had only the one room. He
shared the bathroom. I knew the joys of that. There was a
small closet and a smaller bureau. Most of what was once
in Carroll's cheap bureau and small closet were thrown into
the cardboard suitcase. Most of that was now all over the
floor. The only thing still in the closet was the wonderful
green suit he was wearing the day I fed him Old Crow for
breakfast.

I wouldn't of taken it either.

What was I looking at here? The killer took the risk
of taking the body somewhere else. Why? So the murder
wouldn't be discovered for some time. How long? My best
guess: for as long as it took him to leave town.

With so little time to figure and to work, where do you
stash an entire human body?

Standing in the middle of a room that could of been back
in sunny Stapleton except for the pale green walls and the
great view, I gave it what I called serious "thought." In other
words, I imagined myself the killer with a fresh dead body
at my feet. I put myself into the mind of the man who did
whatever he did to Goose.

OK, so now I'm the killer.

As the killer, I knew what I knew because I'd hidden here
and there, leaping about in the shadows. From the shadows,
I'd watched my whole horse race go down, legs and tails and

jockeys flying every which way. How did I feel when I saw the botch Carroll'd made of my simple plan? I felt I should of risked it myself. It couldn't have gone worse. I wished I'd killed him *before* I'd hired him. I had to know him before. To hire Carroll, I must of known Carroll. What I knew now was Goose was not only a failure, he was a live failure. Alive he'd squeal first chance he got. So he couldn't be alive. I could fix that. If I moved fast, I'd get where Goose lived before he did. But I'd heard what that creep Russo'd said to the Willingford dame. He'd be going there too. So I had to clean up. I couldn't let a peeper hand the police real evidence like a real body. So I had to hide it. But where? This was the backstretch of a racetrack. What did it offer? Grain bins were tempting, but everyone would be scooping out grain real soon. Garbage bins were also tempting, but they were too far away.

Hah! Sam Russo, killer, got it. Flo always called me a "cunning little squat"—truth was, she was right. The cunning little squat suddenly knew where he'd stash Carroll Goose in a hurry. I'd put him to bed where he could slumber for ages—or long enough for me to make myself scarce. How long before someone noticed?

Not in his bed. Goose was supposed to be alive and working for his pay. His boss would come looking. In some other bed, of course, one in some other room for seasonal workers.

The building had three floors. There were maybe six rooms per floor. The place wasn't full. Anyone working the backstretch knew that. So that's where he was. There was nowhere else to put the poor egg.

Me as me, I was out Carroll's door and checking the other doors.

First door to the right, locked. First door to the left, locked. Second door to the right, unlocked. I opened it slowly. Could be somebody left in the world trusting enough to keep his door unlocked. Or he forgot. Not likely either way. I thumbed a match. Got enough light to see the place was exactly the same place as Carroll's was, except the single bed was on the opposite side of the room. There was someone in the bed.

Brother, was he in for a surprise if he was alive. If he wasn't, well, bingo.

Bingo.

Poor old Carroll Goose. Covered up so nobody'd think to bother if they did happen to look in. Just another rummy sleeping off another rummy night. Shades down on the one window. I would of locked the door, and so would the big guy, but there was no key. Management probably kept the key, only gave it out with the room.

Match burned down to nothing, I thumbed another.

Looking down at his poor kewpie doll head on its poor black and purple neck, I thought: well, two good things, no more spending his life having to write Goose on checks and registers and no poor dame ever having to call herself Mrs. Goose.

But the first thing I thought was shame on Goosie for trying to fix a race. And then I remembered Carroll Goose couldn't tell the rear end of a horse from his own. It meant nothing to him. And now nothing meant much to him and never would again. That's what taking a life means. I saw it over and over on Luzon. Men with dreams and feelings and sweethearts and even a couple with a talent or two, and then there was nothing. All of it gone forever. Who had the right to take all that away—even from a schnook like Goose?

If the big guy was strong enough to stuff a ham sandwich down Babe Duffy's throat and hold it there long enough for Duffy to die, meanwhile dealing with Jane, and he was strong enough to get Walker to a lake and keep him under while he drowned, and he was strong enough to hold up McBartle, walking him doped and legless out the door of the Grand Union Hotel, then he was more than strong enough to strangle Carroll Goose. No muss, no fuss, no noise.

I covered the poor sap up again, patted his still warm shoulder.

"You just rest there for awhile, fella. I'll be back to get you when the race is run."

40

You'd think it was time to go to the police. I had an almost
doped horse worth a whole lot of money now being guarded
round-the-clock, I had a sapped groom in the hospital, I had
a dead body left tucked up nicely in bed.

I wasn't going to the police.

I knew what would happen if I went to the police. The
cases of the three dead jockeys were officially closed. They'd
been closed before I ever got off the ferry from Staten Island
much less off the train from Manhattan. The local flatfoots
just hadn't gotten round to admitting it yet.

What would happen was the corpse of Carroll Goose
would get hauled off to the morgue, get charged postmortem
with fixing a race, and I'd get drilled for hours about how
come I knew he was going to do it and why didn't I report
the body, not to mention how did I know where to find it
in the first place? Mrs. Willingford was too important, too
connected and too rich to drill. So I'd get a double dose. Did
I kill him? Somebody did. Witness the obvious prints on his
neck. Did I expect them to believe Carroll Goose, security
guard, tossed his own room, then went off to find a neater
one so he could strangle himself in nicer surroundings?

I wouldn't get charged with his murder, not with Mrs.
Willingford coming to bat for me (she would, right?) but
they'd run me out of town on the proverbial rail.

So, no—no calling the police. Not even Lino for advice.
I already knew what Lino's advice would be. *Amscray the hell
outta that town right this minute, Russo, and get your tail back here
where you belong, solving my cases.*

All I could do and do fast was search Carroll's room for
evidence. Anything would do since so far, aside from Jane,
my guy hadn't left any evidence.

Sure enough, I couldn't find a thing in the room Goose

died in that pointed at anything except Goose trying to pack in a hurry. No blood, no bullet casings, no piece of the killer's shirt or pants or hanky caught on something sharp. Nothing sharp to get caught on. No butts or spent matches. No matchbook with the name of a place the killer hung out. If there was hair or spit or sweat, what would I do with it?

There had to be fingerprints, but I didn't have the equipment for that kind of thing. All I could do in the fingerprint department was make sure I hadn't left any of my own.

I wasn't looking for who did it. I *knew* who did it. Hell, Mrs. Willingford said *she* knew who did it, and I was willing to believe she did. She sure knew Ace Admiral was going to be drugged and when. She said she also knew why, and I believed that too. Mrs. Willingford was a complex piece of goods; it was all I could do to keep up with her. I wasn't calling her Lois though. Besides being Superman's girl when he was wearing skintight everything, plus cape—and what *was* the cape for; never could figure that one out—Lois was the name of one of my worst tormentors back at the Home. Three years older than my "crowd" and mean as a baboon. The party we had the day old Lois got old enough to get the boot was two days long. No, I was looking for anything I could find to take to the police—*if* I ever found myself going to the police—to prove who killed Carroll Goose. Which didn't prove he'd killed anyone else but Goose, but hey, it was a start.

I had to hand it to myself. I'd had work before, small time stuff, the "pro bono" tag alongs with Lino, but when Sam Russo takes on his first solo murder case, right out of the gate, it's a doozy.

I'd left Carroll Goose to his "big sleep," and was back under the Saratoga stars. I wasn't getting any sleep tonight. But what to do now?

If I faced down the guy who would kill three jockeys in what's called "cold blood"—one in broad daylight—knife a dog, dope a horse, and then strangle the schmuck he'd hired to do the doping, I wasn't so sure I wouldn't wind up getting dead too.

He could also laugh in my face. Where was my proof?

I knew where my proof was. She was sleeping in Hank Hanson's bedroom not more than a hundred yards from where I was standing.

That's what I was doing next. I was going to Hank's.

My luck was in. After three in the morning, and Hank was still awake. So was his assistant Maisie. They had to be with a horse suffering from Rotation. Rotation is the separation at the toe of the hoofwall from the bone and is a sure sign of laminitis. Because it was serious, or could wind up serious, this was one of the first things I ever learned around horses.

I stood quietly and watched.

Hank and Maisie were in the process of stabilizing the ailing horse, a nice little bay gelding who was trembling with fear and pain. Whatever they called him on the racetrack, Hank called him Max.

"S'okay, Max. You'll be fine. You'll be swell. You'll be knee deep in high green grass before you know it. That's right, boy, keep still, keep really still so Maisie and I can tighten this strap. Good boy, such a good boy."

I'd never witnessed a more gentle caring touch than Hank's, unless it was the night he saved Jane. But with Jane, he was working fast and he was working without hope. With Max, he had time and I could tell he had hope.

Max calmed before my eyes. His ears straightened, his eyes grew brighter, he even reached forward to nibble Hank's hand. I hadn't noticed before, but Hank's wrist was bandaged. Came with the job, naturally. Not all his patients were Max.

It took some time, waiting for Hank to hear me, but when the time came—Maisie was outside for a minute, getting rid of the mess of trimming a horse's hoof; Hank was washing his hands—I said, "Hank? Can I just have a peek at her?"

He glanced up and smiled.

"Sure. She's still doped, but her signs are all good. Door to my bedroom is that one."

He was pointing at the only door in or out of the room

that wasn't white. It was a light brown natural wood door with a crystal doorknob.

Hank's private room surprised me. The walls were covered in framed photos but not the same photos that cluttered the walls of the Saratoga Jockey Club where Harold George Whitman held forth. These were photos of the horses Hank'd saved. On the surface of his bureau and desk were more, framed and displayed like they'd be on the top of a great big grand piano in some famous person's great big famous house, all studio shots of their famous friends.

These were of more horses, a dog or two, a cat, a parrot. Gifts from grateful owners and trainers, most of 'em. There were halters with brass nameplates, horseshoes, winner's cups, crops, saddle blankets.

I wondered where Jane's photo would go.

I paused for a minute before walking slowly over to Hank's bed. It was a big bed, nicely made, its white tufted bedspread matching the white tufted pillowcases. And in the middle, still wrapped in a woolen car blanket, lay a smallish dog.

Jane looked like a mummy.

I slowly walked to the edge of the bed. Being quiet was easy. Hank had a figured carpet in his private room deep enough for a turf race.

All I did then was stare down at her. I thought about life, about how precious it was, about how whoever you were or whatever you were, you'd fight for it. I couldn't think of a life that had fought harder than Jane. For love, she fought for Babe's. To live, she fought for her own. Jane didn't love much, but what she loved, she'd die for.

I never thought I could care for a dog, but I was falling for this one. The idea that she could die shook me right down to the bone.

"One tough cookie, eh Sam?"

Hank was standing in his own doorway looking at me looking at Jane.

"None tougher, Hank."

"I can't bear to see 'em suffer. I can't bear what men do to animals."

"S'why you're a vet."

"No. Not really. Not at first. I became a vet because first I wanted to be in medicine. But I didn't have whatever it took to be a doc." His glasses had slipped to the end of his nose. The only thing that kept them from falling off was a quick reflex and wide nostrils. "That was money and time, but it was also maybe not enough brains."

"I believe the money and the time. But you got the brains."

"Thanks, Sam. I didn't think so back then. It took a few years to figure out it takes just as much brains to be a vet, only people don't know it. What I really learned the long hard way was what vets really had to do. Doctors don't give up on patients no one has a use for. They don't put down a man with a broken leg. Unless they're Nazis, they don't send undesired humans to slaughterhouses. God, Sam, we're surrounded by horses, beautiful horses, more beautiful, the worst of 'em, than most guys walking around. But they don't win enough, they're so much meat, even the big names. They start to lose, it's over. Stallions too, and broodmares. Their foals don't come up to snuff, that's all she wrote. As for the low end, the hard knocking claimers— "

"Like Carl Hessing's."

"Yeah, like his."

Hank's voice had gotten low. What he was saying was said with a kind of growling passion I'd never heard before, not from him. To me, Hank Hanson was as ugly as a wart hog, but as sweet as Betty Grable. Just not now.

Jane opened her eyes.

"Hank! She's looking at me, Hank!"

He moved fast, fast enough to see I was right, before she closed them again. I put out my hand to touch her and when I did, she'd tried to lick me. It was a feeble effort, but she tried. Jane, who had no time for anyone but Babe Duffy, tried to lick my hand.

I was big baby enough to weep.

Hank took me by the shoulders, began gently leading me back to the door. "You can see her later, word of honor. But right now she needs all the rest she can get. She's not out of the woods, Sam, not by a long shot."

I pulled away. "Let me stay a little longer, Hank. I haven't seen her since... since... "

"Sure. But not too long."

I sat back down on the bed. Hank left the door open and went back to tending Max. I got to thinking about dogs. I never thought I could care for a dog. Sam Russo loved horses, he didn't like dogs. Especially a dog like Jane was a dog. Dogs should be big. Men had big dogs. Only dames liked dogs like Jane. Duffy's mother probably gave him Jane.

She didn't open her eyes again. But her breathing was deep and easy. I imagined my life from now on. I was going to own a dog.

I took to looking around the room again, all those pictures of animals, the neat bed, the nice carpet, the bit of dark blue material sticking out from under the bed.

I leaned over for a better look, then farther over.

The bit of dark blue was a brand new delivery uniform.

I was off the bed and on my knees. The uniform was stuffed under the bed like you'd stuff something you wanted rid off, something you didn't want to see. Something you probably expected to get rid of when you had the time. I pulled it out a bit. It was covered in drying blood. Farther back, up against the wall, was a shoe, one of those two-toned correspondence shoes which are usually black and white or brown and white. This one was red and white. The other shoe must be under the bloody delivery outfit.

I pushed the uniform under the bed, far enough so the blue was out of sight.

As a vet, Hank always wore a shabby white coat over an old grey shirt tucked into a pair of older brown slacks. His shoes were just as shabby.

From one second to the next, I had a headache.

41

Back under the suddenly ominous stars, I walked away from Hank Hanson's little clinic with its private bedroom, its photos on every wall of the animals he'd saved, and his bed. My head ached. My legs were stiff. I was dizzy. And I was thinking furiously.

It was Hank. It wasn't Hank. How could it be Hank Hanson?

Would my old friend Hank, who cared more about animals than he did about humans—something we had in common along with Mrs. Willingford—deliberately set out to kill a dog? Hank didn't kill dogs. He didn't kill bugs if he noticed 'em on his wall or under his shoe. Hank saved animals—or tried his damndest to.

What about the uniform and the shoe? Someone else stuffed them under his bed? Oh sure, and I really *was* Robert Mitchum. I couldn't believe it. I wouldn't believe it. I hated believing it. I *did* believe it.

Why didn't he get rid of the uniform? Why didn't he sink the shoes? He knew where the lake was.

He *could* of ripped off the uniform anywhere from the pink hotel on Case Street to the track. It wasn't far. He was covered in blood. I thought of the neighborhood and the hour. In the dark, who'd notice the blood? In the dark, what was more noticeable: a quickly moving man in a uniform or a man struggling out of a uniform?

In that neighborhood the trash bins were behind the houses. On the track, the uniform would of been found in a matter of hours if he'd used their bins.

Some killers liked to keep souvenirs. Were these his? Not likely. It made more sense to think he intended to destroy them. But it was the season. He barely had time to sleep, much less run around looking for a great place to ditch evidence no one was looking for.

No one, that is, but me. He knew I didn't suspect him. He knew I thought he was not only a good guy, but a great guy.

Even now, staggering from one shed row to the next, I thought he was a great guy. He'd saved Jane's life.

Oh, hell, he also tried to take Jane's life.

By now, I was just going somewhere, anywhere, nowhere. By now, my ears were ringing and my head was pounding so hard I could barely think.

This case was killing me. Whose wise idea was it to become a private dick? Dumbest idea I ever had.

It couldn't be Hank. But Hank had a new dark blue and bloody delivery outfit. He had a shoe.

All right, but if Hank'd really gone to my pink hotel to kill Jane, he'd never make such a mess of it. If I knew Hank, and by now I wasn't sure I knew Hank, or anyone else, he would of brought a syringe full of something to put her quietly and painlessly "out of her misery."

It didn't take much to see the idea was a simple one. No one would know he was the track vet. He was a delivery man. He'd come to deliver an easy death to a dog. But it didn't go like that. When Jane saw a strange man open my door and slowly approach her with his compassionate needle, he got a reaction he hadn't prepared for. Maybe Jane smelled his intention, maybe she knew about needles.

I remembered his bandaged wrist.

I remembered she didn't need to smell or sense anything. She got a whiff of the guy who killed Babe Duffy.

Fuck. If he killed Duffy, he killed them all.

Jane went for him—again—with everything she had.

His syringe was suddenly useless. The quick and painless death wasn't going to happen. It was Hank on the receiving end. That would explain the kitchen knife and the mess. Stabbing a fast and furious dog over and over must have been a nightmare for a man who'd spent his life saving animals.

I practically fell down on a stool near an open stall. I sat there trying to breathe. I sat there trying to keep going. I sat there for some time before I noticed I was sitting outside the stall of Fleeting Fancy. Fancy's chestnut head with its off-center star was over her door nodding at me. I nodded back.

Mrs. and Mr. Willingford's gorgeous filly was wide awake on the eve of the Travers. It didn't matter. She wouldn't be running in it.

I sat there and shivered. I'd thought I knew who my killer was. Mrs. Willingford thought she knew. I'd bet anything we both had the same man in mind. We were both wrong.

I put my head between my knees and quietly cried.

I loved Hank Hanson. Why would Hank try and kill my dog? There was only one reason. He did it to save his own life.

How Jane could threaten his life was as obvious as the red and white shoe under his bed, as certain as Citation winning another race. Because it was Hank who killed the jockeys.

But if he needed her dead, why try to save her?

Because I'd called him to the scene of the crime. Because he had to come and he had to make it look good for me when he got there. So why not finish the job while I was off getting fired? Because he was Hank Hanson, and he couldn't keep hurting her. Because he didn't believe she stood a chance anyway. To him, she was already dead. She was just taking her time getting around to accepting it.

But she still hadn't died. Because she was Jane. But also because he was Hank. He couldn't help himself. It was in his heart to save, not to kill.

I remembered what I hadn't noticed at the time, the look on his face when I called out to him, when I told him she'd opened her eyes. His eyes weren't full of satisfied joy; they were empty with fear.

She was supposed to die. He'd done all he could, but she was supposed to die.

I lifted my head. Above me, Fancy snorted.

I stood and held her head. Holding her, her scent in my nose, I whispered in her ear. "If Hank Hanson killed three young jockeys, if the only person who could pin it on him was a dog, he has no choice. He failed the first time. He has to try again. He still has to kill Jane."

My dog was helpless, swaddled on his bed. His bed was in his private bedroom. He could inject her at any moment. S'why he'd said she "wasn't out of the woods." He said that so I wouldn't be surprised when she didn't make it. He said it so I'd know it was on the cards. So that I'd expect it.

I used my sleeve to wipe my eyes.

I said, "PIs don't cry."

Fleeting Fancy shook her head. It was our secret.

42

I was up and away from Fleeting Fancy's stall like she'd of been up and out of the gate if Mrs. Willingford hadn't scratched her from the Travers.

Less than an hour and the sky over Saratoga would lighten. Less than an hour and the whole backstretch would come awake, every man, woman, horse and a whole host of animal chums. The noise, the color, the life—I loved it so. But now?

Less than an hour.

There were no choices left. I had to do what I had to do, and I had to do it immediately.

Peeking round the corner of a shed row at Hank's clinic, I saw Maisie standing in front of the slowly closing door. I heard her say, "I could stay if you needed me, Mr. Hanson. I could— "

Hank said, "Max is fine. I won't leave his side. You know I won't."

And then he shut the door in her face. We both knew he would never leave an animal in as much trouble as Max was. But only I knew he'd find just enough time to deal with Jane. If she could lick a hand, what else could she do?

Maisie went one way, I went another. I was slipping in and out of shadows to get to the back of Hank's clinic. In the back was his bedroom and in the back wall of his back bedroom was a good sized window. Summer in Saratoga Springs meant open windows. It also meant closed screens. It was the screen I was thinking about. That, and getting in and out without his hearing me. Or his walking in just as I was climbing in.

The window wasn't high. It was a normal height from the scrub grass that grew against the back of the clinic. What I needed was something to stand on. I also needed something to pry open the screen. What I needed most was luck. Hank couldn't see the Titanic without his glasses, but his hearing was just peachy.

In and around horse barns you can find pretty much anything. I found a wooden feed bucket. I also found a hoof knife. The hoof knife was just the thing to pry open the screen window, or failing that, to cut the screen out of its frame.

I knew how to be sneaky. The way I was raised, no one but Paul and Lino were as sneaky as me. I'd swear on oath in court I was sneakiest of all. It was all a matter of brains. Lino didn't have any and mine were better than Paul's. That was my opinion and I'd never found reason to change it. Climbing in or out of a window was a snap. Just so long as nothing went wrong. And things could go wrong. It was a law of nature: something usually gummed up the works. A groom coming round the back of the clinic for a predawn piss. One of the "companions" of any of one of a hundred high bred horses making a fuss over finding me. Most likely of all, Hank choosing his moment exactly when I was choosing mine.

Turning over the bucket and placing it under the window was easy. Stepping up on it was easy. Seeing into the bedroom was easy. Jane was still there, swaddled just as I'd left her. The door to Hank's bedroom was closed. My dog was alone. She could be dead, but I doubted it. Hank would never take the risk while Maisie was still around. To anyone else, he could say he was giving the dog a sedative, but Maisie would know what she was looking at.

Hank wasn't a dummy. Why do something when anyone was still around? He'd wait until he was nice and alone and safe. Me, I'd also wager anything, any damn thing at all, he was out with Max wrestling with his conscience. If he killed the jocks, he must of had a good reason—Hank Hanson was a good man. I thought so, even now. But Jane, an animal, a dog—the only reason he had for this particular kiss off was no better than any other killer's. To save himself.

The screen came away pretty easy and about as easy I lowered it to the ground beneath me. Now it was nothing more than hoisting myself through the window. My childhood was all about hoisting myself through windows. I did it to listen to Mister's radio. I did it to escape my happy home. I did it out a small bathroom window and down a homemade rope. On radio days, later I'd shimmy back up again.

Hank's window was child's play. I made noise, couldn't be helped, but not much noise. I was a pro.

I'd brought a canvas hay bag—Fleeting Fancy's spare. I'd emptied it, then slung it over my shoulder by its strap; it was something to carry Jane away in since I hoped climbing *out* the window would be just as easy as climbing *in*. Truth was, out couldn't be as easy. I had to drop down onto the upturned bucket without tipping it and I had to do that soundlessly carrying a dog in a hay bag.

Not much of a chance of that. I was no ballerina and Jane wasn't going to help.

Too bad. What had to be, had to be. If I got caught, it was me against Hank. If it came to that, well, it came to that.

I was in the room. Nothing to it. I'd been quiet as— not a mouse. Mice could make a hell of a racket, skittering about, gnawing things, squeaking. I'd been as quiet as Sam Russo going hand over hand down the side of his "home" to listen to *Amos 'n' Andy*.

No gun in my pocket. A good thing because the last thing I wanted to do was shoot an old friend. It didn't matter what he'd done. And a bad thing because my old friend might have a gun in his pocket, or a hypodermic needle full of something that could fell a musk ox. Right there I realized there was no need for a "big man" to overpower McBartle or Walker or, most especially, Duffy. All it took was them trusting him and his bringing along a nice little needle.

There was no point in doing what I was doing slowly. Best to get it done as fast as possible. I was by the side of Hank's bed, gathering up Jane, tucking her and all her bandages into the hay bag, then just as quickly draping the strap of the bag over my head so it wouldn't fall off my shoulder.

I was halfway back to the window when the door opened. I froze, leg in the air.

"What are you doing, Sam?"

"Saving my dog."

"You can't save your dog. You're not a vet."

We were both talking double time and double talk. I was moving again as fast as I could, climbing out his window. He was also moving, coming just as fast across the short expanse of his bedroom. No time to feel around for the feed bucket. It was hold Jane close and jump or Hank'd have a chance to grab the hay bag. Or better still, stick the needle he was holding into me. Then simply shoot me full of whatever was in it.

"You'll kill her, Sam. She can't take the jolt when you land. And you won't land well."

He was right. I probably couldn't take it either. So I'd be doing his job for him, plus breaking a leg or two.

"Thanks for your help, Hank. The check's in the mail."

And then I jumped.

43

I didn't drop her and I didn't fall. I did hurt my back but so? I was on the ground and running, it didn't matter where just so long as Hank couldn't follow.

But he wouldn't follow.

The horses were waking up. Saratoga Race Track was coming alive on Travers Day. How would it look to have Hank Hanson, track veterinarian, chasing me and my mummified dog, yelling, "Come back! You both need a nice little shot! Won't hurt at all!"

I knew where I was going. I was going to find Mrs. Willingford. If anyone could put Jane somewhere Hank would never find her—or if he did find her, he couldn't get into the place—it was Mrs. Joker Willingford. I also had a lot to tell her. I doubt she'd believe me—who could believe me? Hank Hanson, all around good guy, a cold blooded murderer?

But she would believe me, eventually. First, of course, it would help if I believed me. I think I did. I didn't want to, but the terrible truth was, I did believe me.

Once all that was done, I had to figure out what to do about it. Not to mention answering another burning question.

Did Hank Hanson kill Carroll Goose after Goose failed to dope Ace Admiral?

Hank couldn't of. Right about the time Goose was getting himself throttled, Hank Hanson was either with Maisie tending to Max, the gelding with Rotation, or tending to the sapped groom.

So who hired Carroll Goose to dope Ace Admiral and when Carroll failed, who killed him and hid the body?

Christ on a cracker. There were two killers at Saratoga Race track.

One last twister for my poor overworked brain. If Hank Hanson killed those three young jockeys—and he did— *why?*

I hadn't a clue. Well, I had a clue and its name was Jane. But Jane could only tell me what she knew about Babe. The other deaths and all three motives were pure supposition. As I'd already figured out, I had no case even if Jane, once again feeling her oats, bit Hank. What did it prove? Animals loved Hank. What it proved was that Jane was crackers.

I hadn't sat through all those movies and eaten all that popcorn for nothing. Unless my old friend Hank was as fruity as a nut cake, he must of had a motive. But so far only he knew what it was. I was supposed to be a private investigator. But all I really had to do was find out who did it. Why was someone else's problem.

Wasn't it?

I didn't know. And it was killing me.

But before I ran around messing with any of that, I ducked into an empty stall of sweet smelling hay. I wanted to see Jane, to feel her breath on my hand, to know she was still alive.

Aces! My dog was not only alive, she was awake. Not only was she awake, she was struggling in her swaddling.

"Jane, hey Jane," I said. I didn't know what else to say. I'd spoken to a lotta horses, some who listened, some who didn't, and some who bit me once they understood what I meant. Exercising all those two-year-olds, a man could get pretty raw—in more ways than one. But before Jane, dogs and I were not on speaking terms. A kid doesn't grow up in the "Home" surrounded by pets. Unless he counted the rats and the cockroaches.

"It's Sam, Jane. You remember me?"

I got stared at for a moment, and then she opened her mouth and from it came a small yodel. And then another. And another. And then she tried to lick me again.

Not counting my weep for Hank, for the third time in less than a month, I came close to bawling like a baby.

Would Bogie cry? Would Cagney? Would Mitchum? Maybe not. But would Russo? He would. He had. And he did.

It was time to be up and doing. Who knew if Hank had another jock in his sights.

"We'll have you talking and biting in no time," I said, touching her gently on her nose.

Then I hung her once again round my neck in her hay bag and we were on our way to the one place I knew I'd find Mrs. Willingford. If she wasn't there yet, she would be.

Until then, Jane and I would wait with Fleeting Fancy.

Turns out, we didn't have to wait for anyone. Scratch Mason, Fancy's trainer, made his entrance before us. I'd heard him from a shed row away swearing at his exercise rider, tossing oats around, kicking up straw, and all the while keeping up a loud and colorful commentary about "fucking owners."

As for Fancy, you'd think she was a member of *Our Gang*. She was snorting and curling her upper lip and tossing her head. No doubt she'd seen Scratch like this before and would see him like it again. As her trainer kicked her straw around, she reached out and snipped off a thick thatch of his hair as gently as a good barber. Scratch was too outraged to notice. But he would. That much hair? He would.

The fucking owner in question, Mrs. Willingford, was also already there. Dressed for a swell day at the races, including a hat shaped like an orange waffle iron stuck to the side of her head, she'd turned out the groom and was currying Fancy all by herself. The way she was going about it said something was on her mind and that something was supremely irritating.

I said, "Mrs. Willingford?"

And the way she spun away from Fleeting Fancy and towards me, made me think it might be me. Holding Jane close, I backed up.

"Ah, Russo. Guess what that ass of a Jockey Club bozo said to me. Go on, guess."

"Something along the lines of what Scratch is saying?"

"What Scratch is— ? Forget Scratch. He's not important."

"Forget Whitman. He's not important. We have to

talk."

"Forget Whitman! What the hell is that hanging round your neck? Have you stolen a baby?"

"It's Jane. Shut up and come over here."

"Shut— ?"

"—up. You heard me."

Fifteen minutes later, Mrs. Willingford was sitting on the edge of the feed trough in Fancy's stall. I was sitting on a bale of hay. Scratch had taken Fancy out for an early morning workout mostly to keep her from biting off any more of his hair. Jane was in my arms taking some sort of meaty gruel from some sort of bottle thing orphaned foals fed from.

Mrs. Willingford had listened to me without a word. That in itself surprised me. Now she was thinking without a word. Watching her think was kind of interesting. She made no sound, yet her painted mouth moved constantly.

She spoke. She said, "But I was *sure* it was— "

"You and me both. But it wasn't. Not the jockeys anyway."

"But that's why I hired his damn jockey. So he'd be close all the time and maybe I could find some sort of proof. And that's why I scratched Fancy. So he wouldn't profit by what he'd done."

"He didn't kill those kids."

"Right. So fuck me. How do I make it up to him? Both of them?"

"Both of them?"

"Of course. Toby Tyrrell just lost the mount. He's only just up from a bug boy. It was his big break as a real jock."

"Give him Fancy's next race. Tell everyone. He'll be in demand just for you and Joker using him. It'll season 'im."

She gave me a look I hadn't caught from her before. I took it as a compliment.

I said, "As for his agent, he's not in the clear. Not in my book."

"But if he didn't kill the jockeys— ?"

"He did something. I just have to work out what that was and how it all connects."

"What is it you think he did?"

"Who tried to dope Ace Admiral?"

"Oh, that's right. Who did?"

"This is the part I haven't told you yet."

"My god, there's more?"

"Oh yeah. Lots more. Carroll Goose tried to get at the horse. But we ruined that by turning up, thanks to you— "

She patted my knee. It was a long cry from what we'd done at the Grand Union Hotel.

"So he ran. By the time I caught up with him, he was dead."

"You're not serious? An accident?"

"You're kidding?"

"Only hoping."

"You can forget hope. Hope is for suckers. He got strangled. After that, whoever strangled him, hid the body."

"And you found it. Aren't you clever."

I gave her a look like the kind she was usually dishing out. For once, it worked. She lowered her eyes. And then she raised them, full of her usual fire.

"Hand Jane over. I'll send for a groom to bring a platoon of grooms. She'll be going somewhere no one will ever guess or get to. I'll call our personal vet. As for you— "

"As for me?"

"As for you, from this minute on you work for me and Joker. Don't tell me what you cost. I don't give a good goddamn. All I care about is it's your job to prove all this."

She was right. It was. Great.

As I walked out into the sweet morning of a great racetrack, I left behind the scent of gardenias and musk. Mixed in with hay and horseshit and a smallish dog.

44

I had about as much idea how to prove Hank Hanson killed three young jockeys as I knew how to crochet doilies. As for *why* he killed 'em, that was a real stumper. Why made as much sense as a doily or one of Mrs. Willingford's hats. But I knew *how* he killed them. No need to be big or tall to overpower any of 'em. He had his little syringe and he had their trust. He was Hank Hanson, the track veterinarian. Who would fear him?

All he needed was to get close enough, then the tiniest prick of a needle—they were out for as long as he wanted 'em to be. Which was, apparently, forever.

Manny Walker didn't even need the needle. He'd already rendered himself senseless. Just a matter of slipping into the jockey's doss house when all the rest were asleep, slinging a drunk as small as a big kid over a shoulder, grabbing his swim trunks, then draping him over the back of a horse. After that, it was a nice dark ride to the lake. One way for Walker.

A few days later, over at the Grand Union Hotel, Matt McBartle was probably sound asleep. Even that late, finding Hank at his door would ring no bells. Hiya Hank, he might of said, bit late to come calling. And Hank would say whatever Hank had planned on saying—probably some baloney about a horse he was meant to ride getting sick—and in went the needle at precisely the right time. In his case, Hank needed him to be able to walk, so the dose had to be smaller. He'd half carried the second jock out of the hotel in the dead of night, Hank wearing a pair of ridiculous shoes that were bound to distract any witnesses, get the doped jock into his nice new car, and drive him towards Mrs. Willingford's hangout, *Haven's Inn*. This one took a little risk. Hank had to be sure of two things. One, that McBartle would die. And two, that the car would hit hard enough to look like the crash

killed him. If I were Hank—which sadly wasn't all that hard
to imagine; a war could do that to a guy—what I'd do is kill
McBartle before the crash, hit him with something where
it would look like the crash did it. Then drive into the tree
myself. I'd really hit the pedal, get up speed, then jump the
hell out at the perfect moment. Or prop the gas pedal to
the floor at low speed and jump out. Only had to gather up
McBartle's body and arrange it in the driver's seat, and fix
the gas pedal.

From there it was only about a two mile walk back to
the track.

Then came Babe Duffy. This was the one where Hank
made his big mistake. He killed Duffy with his dog there.
Strolling up in broad daylight, saying hi or whatever, probably
getting asked to have a sit while Babe ate his lunch. Then,
again timing the moment, out with the needle, followed by
the unpleasant matter of stuffing the ham sandwich down
Babe's throat. He'd of choked drugged or not. Trouble with
that one was, Jane got to Hank.

Didn't save Babe Duffy though. Hank should of killed
Jane then and there while he had the chance. But Hank
loved animals.

As for the other little problem, I knew exactly why
Carroll Goose was killed. Basically, Carroll Goose couldn't
keep his trap shut and the guy who hired him to dope Ace
Admiral knew it too. The plan'd been simple. It was based
on the laws of chance. Fancy was a great filly. She was aces.
On her best day she could beat anything. But as Paul and
I were always saying, along with everyone else who hung
around the ponies, she could just as easily lose. There was
no telling how a horse would run from race to race. Win
once as a huge long shot, lose the next as the chalk. Chalk,
like I'd said to the guy with teeth like piano keys, meant the
favorite. It came from back when bookies chalked up the
changing odds on black boards. So the plan was to reduce
the odds by making sure the chalk, which happened to be
Ace Admiral, was so doped up he couldn't win a race with
one of Mark Twain's frogs. But thanks to chance or bad luck
or some sort of hoodoo voodoo the plan flopped because

the surprising Mrs. Willingford suspected this might happen to Ace Admiral. Being Mrs. Willingford, she acted on her hunch. And me being me, I got dragged along. Which meant we arrived just after Goose sapped the groom, but before he could inject the horse with some sort of tranquilizer. Phenothiazine. Lots of horse racing crooks had gone down for phenothiazine.

So Goose got caught in the act and Goose ran. And I saw Goose run so I chased him. I lost him but who could miss the smell? A rummy like Carroll Goose? If I'd been down with flu, I could still smell him.

But the big guy was watching. He wouldn't just trust Goose to get it right, or even, come to think, to do it at all. So he was watching. And Goose knew he was watching. He'd probably been told he'd be watched.

That meant the big man knew things had gone all to hell and blooey. At that point, what else could he do? Go see his hired boob before anyone else saw him, me for instance, and shut him up. Knowing my guy, I bet he didn't intend to kill Goose. Knowing Goose, I'd bet he got himself killed by his own big fat mouth.

I could hear him now. "But I got seen, ya hear me? So now I gotta get away. Doping a horse in a big race gets a guy in whole lotta dutch. I heard things. I been keeping my ears open. So maybe, say just maybe, if I go to the track guys and confess, alls I'll do is lose my job. Hey, the season is over up here, all but the shoutin'. I'm gonna hafta find another job anyways. Yeah, that's what I'll do. If I don't, I could do time or something. Won't I do time?"

What could my guy do? If Goose talked, the big man'd lose his reputation. Without his good name, he didn't have a job. So he tried to talk Goose out of his usual bone-headed idea. All Goose had to do, he would of told him, was to keep his mouth shut and deny deny deny. He wasn't caught, was he? No. He got away. No one could prove it was him in the stall. But no, Carroll Goose wouldn't listen. Goose was scared. And time was fleeting, just like the big man's dream. So he hit Goose and when Goose hit back, which he was bound to do, the big man probably found himself with his hands round the dummy's throat squeezing the life out of him.

And there he was standing over a dead body. He wasn't Adlai E. Stevenson who could of talked his way out of anything, but he wasn't Goose either. Goose talked his way right into things, usually for the worst. So the big man hid the body. He'd expect he was safe until it was found, and by then, like most everyone working the track, he'd be gone, working some other track.

Some track as far from Saratoga as he could get.

But for now, he had to get through the Travers Stakes Day. If he fled too soon, it wouldn't look good, not to anyone keeping an eye out. He had a bunch of eyes watching. But if he went about his usual business, who would suspect him? Of what? Ace Admiral was fine. Goose wouldn't be missed until he began to stink up his room.

The big man must already know the horse he was counting on to save his butt was scratched. So he was probably doing what Goose would of been doing if Goose'd had a brain in his head. He'd be in bed. He probably hadn't slept. He'd probably been thinking. All night I bet he lay there, planning out every move he had to make next.

He'd get up at his usual time. It was the biggest day in Saratoga's racing season. The Travers Stakes was going off; he had to be there. He had to look like every other race goer looked, do what every other race goer did. Being a professional, he had to carry that off too—do his job like it was any other race day at any other track.

Like millions of other people, he'd eat his breakfast just like he did every day.

I knew when he ate his bacon and eggs in the morning and I knew where he ate 'em.

No leaving my gun behind this time. A man who killed a man, even if he hadn't planned to, might kill again, even if he didn't want to. The law of self preservation was a strong law, the strongest.

I knew that as well as anyone.

45

I was headed for *The Bent Spoon*. It was across the street from the Grand Union and up a bit, a little place on the corner of Broadway Street and Lake Avenue. *The Bent Spoon*. Odd name for the gaggle of little old ladies who sat at the back poring over their racing forms and who'd bet a buck every other race, if that. Great name for the queer ducks who used it as an eye on Broadway. In front it was all windows and everyone at a window seat was looking for another likely brightly feathered nance. Saratoga in the season attracted fags from Manhattan like Staten Island at any time attracted, well, pretty much nothing.

It was an even better name for the fella who was sitting with his back to the door, his elbows on a checkered table cloth, a pot of tea steaming in front of him, leaning over his own racing form.

Today the Travers was running and I'd bet none of 'em knew Fleeting Fancy was scratched. If they had, the whole place would of been funereal. A filly beating the colts was exactly what the kind of people in *The Bent Spoon* lived for. When they came to the races, that is.

I'd bet my guy knew she was scratched.

Even from the back, it was him all right, nose in the paper with a pencil in one hand and a cigarette in the other.

He was wearing his worst Hawaiian shirt yet—mustard yellow all over with gigantic puce shapes that might have been grey flowers, and then again might have been the world's ugliest mushrooms.

I said, "Mind if I join you?" I was already pulling out a chair and seating myself across from him.

Paul Jarrett looked up, saw who'd taken the liberty, and for the flash of a second, his baby blues widened while the corners of his mouth tightened—until he covered whatever it was he felt with one of his terrific Gable grins.

You had to give it to him, Paul really had a lot of charm.

Funny thing was, even knowing what I knew and having seen what I'd seen, I hated this part. It was *The Maltese Falcon* and Bogie all over again. Hot for the two-timing schemer of a twisted dame, his heart broken but his backbone unbent, when the time comes to turn her in, he does what he has to do—he turns her in. Like he says—well he doesn't say it at all, but like he means: an old friend was an old friend, one he'd grown up with, one he'd climbed down handmade ropes with, one he'd admired, but when a PIs reputation is on the line, it was on the line. Would Bogie pull his hat down over his eyes and his trench coat collar up and just walk away? Would he whistle like it had nothing to do with him? You bet he wouldn't. And neither would Sam Russo.

I picked up a piece of his toast and bit it. Chewing, I said, "I found him, Paul."

"Oh yeah? Found who?"

"Goose."

"Why in the world would you wanna find Goose?"

"To stop what was gonna happen to him. Only I was too late."

"Too late for what?"

"To keep you from killing him."

Paul poured himself some tea. He pointed at the pot. "You want some of this? It's right off the boat from India."

"Coffee's more my speed."

"Suit yourself. But anytime you change your mind." And with that he went right back to his racing form.

"Fleeting Fancy's been scratched."

"I know. I was out at the track at dawn. It was all they were talking about. But there she was, warming up anyway, running away from Ace Admiral in first light. Me and a load of other fellas made a hell of lot of noise when we heard. Bad luck all around and mostly for me. I gotta ask, was it Scratch again?"

"No. Not this time. It was Mrs. Willingford."

"Her! Why? We all saw there was nothing wrong with the horse. It's not raining. Or snowing. It's not even too hot. And after I get my jockey the mount and all. That filly winning would of been the making of me. And Toby Tyrrell too."

"It certainly would of been the saving of you, Paul. They still want their grand?"

"By the end of the day. I told 'em Toby winning the Travers would do it."

"Well, that's not going to happen, is it? You got a nice bolt-hole all picked out?"

"Like I'd tell you. So why'd she scratch?"

"She did it so you wouldn't profit from trying to dope Ace Admiral. Or from choking the life out of Carroll Goose."

Paul finally looked at me. And then he did what I was used to him doing. He put his elbows on the table and leaned in close. "I've taken this pretty well, you comin' in here and ruining my breakfast on a day already pretty much beat to hell. You got proof of all this guff, old friend?"

I looked right back at him like I'd shot a feature film of the main events. Of course I had no proof. "What do you think I'm doing here?"

"Shucking and jiving. If you had proof, you wouldn't be here. The cops would be here."

Good point.

"Haven't gone to the cops yet. Wanted to talk to you first."

"Old times sake, eh Sam?"

"Sort of like that."

Paul laughed, a real laugh. "You really believe all you're saying Sammy, and you can prove it, I'm sure to get some hot tips in the slammer."

"I can really prove all this." I couldn't prove it, and since I couldn't prove it, might as well really go for broke. "I found a witness."

For the first time, shadows darkened the planes of his face. For the first time, it looked like doubt might have entered his heart.

"Fuck you, you fucking snoop. You always been a snoop, all our lives. Funny you being such a great snoop, you never caught on to Mister."

"What do you mean?"

"I knew Mister done your mom since, Jesus, since forever. I even knew which mound we played on was hers."

From one second to the next, things over at our table had turned dark. I wasn't feeling so good, not that I'd begun by feeling good. But now I was feeling bad. Crazy bad. "You knew and you never——."

"Told you? Why should I? I thought it was funny."

I stood so suddenly my chair fell backward, instantly shutting up every startled soul in *The Bent Spoon*. Something had snapped in me, something I didn't know could break. Without thinking twice, I was reaching for my gun, right side jacket pocket.

But Paul beat me to it. He had his own gun. He shot me three times.

I'm pretty sure I only shot him once.

46

I opened my eyes. Blurry. Not getting less blurry. But I knew I wasn't in the Murphy bed in Stapleton. I wasn't in the pink hotel or the Grand Union Hotel. I wasn't in a coffin, buried or unburied. Where the hell was I?

I didn't think I was dead. Wherever dead people wake up, I was sure they didn't have tubes sticking out of them, or Thomas Jefferson Clay's walleyed face a few inches from theirs. Him, I could see.

"What you doing here?"

"Been here off and on ever since I heard."

"Really?"

"Have I ever lied to you? But I was wrong about Mrs. Willingford, and that's a fact."

"That's a fact."

"Mrs. Willingford!" That was Clay doing the yelling. "Sorry, Mr. Russo. She can't hear me, I guess. I'll have to go get her."

Then off he galloped like Bucephalus while I stayed where I was, feeling just fine. Immobile but fine. Must be as doped as Paul meant Ace Admiral to be.

Mrs. Willingford was back with Clay soon enough to make me think she'd been right outside the door.

"You're in a hospital, Sam. The best of everything. You had a close— "

"Who won the Travers?"

"Ace Admiral."

"Damn. We could of won it."

"We?"

"Me and Fancy."

"You'll win the next one. She's entered in the Alabama Stakes."

"The Alabama? But that's just fillies."

"She'll get another chance at the boys. Speaking of boys, Toby's riding. Guess what he told me."

"Can't. Guessers out of order."

"Confessed he knew Paul intended doing something to the Admiral. Said he wasn't worthy of Fancy."

"What'd you say?"

"I said, get yourself a new agent."

And with that I remembered.

"Paul? Is he... did I... ?"

"He is and you didn't. Although he almost did you. Right this minute, he's down the hall. They won't let me pull out his tubes."

I shut up for a minute, getting my bearings. What a dick I was. I hadn't proved anything. Paul gave himself away. Now I was awake, the police were sure to come calling and I'd tell 'em about Goose. They'd go get the dumb slob out of that lonely bed and do what they do to murder victims. But it was the Saratoga cops who'd have to make the case against Paul, not me. Or maybe the guys he owed a grand to would beat 'em to him. I should of felt sorry, but I didn't care much anymore. After all, not so long ago Paul Jarrett was one of my best friends.

Come to that, so was Hank Hanson.

I was losing friends faster than the usual mug at a track lost money.

I should of cared. I didn't care. Maybe that would wear off when the dope wore off. Maybe it wouldn't. Not after what Paul said about my mother.

The case they had against him shooting me was easy. The whole of the café on Broadway Street saw Paul get the draw on me. What I did was in self defense. Of course if he'd waited just a second or two more, the gunfight at *The Bent Spoon* would of been in reverse.

No movie stuff for me. Shot three times but pulling out the drip feed and throwing back the covers so I could crawl out of my death bed and still keep going. I could tell if I tried that, I'd kill myself. So no proving Hank's murders either. The case I was hired to solve, wasn't solved by me. The other case I was hired to solve would have to wait until I was out of a hospital bed. Whenever that might be.

No one but me and Mrs. Willingford and Hank knew about Hank. And Jane.

"Lois, how's Jane?"

If she noticed I'd called her Lois, she didn't make a move to say so, not even a twitch of the eye.

"Jane will live. Just like you. You're meant for each other. Stabbed and shot, and you're still here. Which reminds me."

Mrs. Willingford was in another one of those outfits of hers. Hat like a wagon wheel, suit like a man's including the slacks, shoes like an ancient torture device, mouth like a bleeding heart, and eyes like Boston's. She was reaching into her jacket pocket and pulling out an envelope.

"Hank left this at the Grand Union. They gave it to me to give to you."

I tried but I couldn't reach for it. I knew if I tried, I couldn't read it.

"Read it to me."

Clay was standing behind her. "You want me to leave, Mr. Russo?"

"No. I want us all to hear what he has to say."

Mrs. Willingford said, "The envelope says *For Sam Russo*." And so saying, she slit it open with one of those long lethal nails she had. Then she began reading.

"Dear Sam,

I have to tell somebody why I did what I did. I have to tell someone I'm not a monster. And who better than you who saw what happened in the Philippines?

It was just chance, you see. Chance that brought those three jockeys to Saratoga at the same time and chance that I got the job for the season. Usually, one is riding at a track I'm at, but never all three. I saw it as a sign. I still do.

You know what I feel about people, Sam, and you know what I feel about horses. Those three, no matter how much trainers thought of them or how much the public thought they were great kids, they were cruel. They whipped whatever they rode until it bled. I know. I fixed up a lot of bad cuts. They ruined their mouths. I'd watch them race a two year old and ruin it for life. But they'd win so often, you see, everyone overlooked what they did. I never overlooked it. I watched and I hated them. I knew if I could, one day I'd make them pay. And then this chance came along, maybe the only one I'd ever get. So I took it. And maybe that makes me a monster, playing God like that. But I took it because I had to.

I'd make each one look like an accident. And if that didn't work, who would think of me? I had nothing to gain. Except to rid the racing world of brutes like those kids, the kind who'd go on for years hurting horses.

Funny thing it should be a dog that was my undoing, a dog and an old friend. You are my friend, Sam. And I'm yours. I don't know what I was thinking when I tried for you. Nature kicking in I suppose.

Anyway, I'm sorry for that.

And I'm more sorry than I can ever say for the dog. The dog is why I'm writing this. The dog is why I'm finished.

If you still want to see me, you'll find me at the lake I drowned Manny in. You'll have to dredge a bit. I put a lot of stones in my pockets.

Hank Hanson, veterinarian.'"

Mrs. Willingford put the letter down and looked at me. Clay was right beside her, doing the same thing. What could I say to them? I understood every word he'd written. I thought of Magpie dying with perfect grace just after she'd taken me over an embankment of Japs, machine guns blazing. I thought of some of the guys joking as they ate their own horses. I thought of all those photos on Hank's bedroom wall.

OK, so three murdered kids were going on the books as accidents unless I handed over Hank Hanson's letter. Something in me balked at the idea. Hank paid for what he'd done and what he'd done I'd come real close to doing too as I watched guys kill the horses who'd carried them through fire and back.

The hell with it.

I did get close to a sleek-looking woman and a few rounds of smart and sassy backtalk.

I loved Hank Hanson. After all, he'd saved my dog's life.

"Burn the letter, Mrs. Willingford."

"My thoughts exactly, Mr. Russo."

Enjoying the adventures of Sam Russo, Private Eye?

Turn the page to preview the first chapter of Sam's next case GOOD DOG, BAD DOG ...

GOOD DOG, BAD DOG and other books in the Sam Russo Mystery series are available from:

www.eiobooks.com

And your favorite bookseller.

Follow Ki Longfellow on the Internet:

Blog kilongfellow.wordpress.com
Facebook Ki Longfellow
Twitter @KiLongfellow
Official Website www.kilongfellow.com
Sam Russo www.eiobooks.com/samrusso

It was seven p.m. on a cold evening in early November and I was still in my striped pajamas chain smoking Luckies. Where I was lying was on the old Murphy bed reading Gypsy Rose Lee's *The G-String Murders*. Not bad writing for an ex-stripper. Maybe I should write a book? It beat taking your clothes off for a pack of drooling mugs or getting seriously plugged three times by one of the funniest, most inventive, most adventuresome kids I once called "friend" back in the days of our old alma mater: the Staten Island Home for Children, aka the Staten Island Lock Up for Lost Little Kiddies.

Jane was lying up against my side, her knife wounds healing as well as my bullet holes, but she'd be badly scarred for life. I could hide mine but Jane's would always look like she'd tripped over the railing of the Central Park Zoo's croc exhibit.

Getting shot takes something out of you. I still had no idea if whatever that was had any intention of coming back.

My manly chest looked like a used target. There were three fresh scars from three fresh bullets neatly spaced round where I assumed my heart was. By some strange miracle they'd all missed the bulls-eye.

My brain still worked and my lungs still wheezed—that last part probably came from too many smokes and from running around the Philippine island of Luzon breathing the fumes of war. My legs and arms moved when I wanted them too. Everything worked, though I suppose I could say sleeping was a problem—I was doing maybe too much of it.

I could still talk. Not that I'd done much talking since it happened. Sleeping yes, talking no.

OK, so I was better off than a ton of other guys I'd known

coming through an entire world war. Ironic that back then when all those bullets were aimed my way, they missed. Close to four years worth of 'em and not even a hole in my hat. And then, when the world finally settles down to lick its wounds and rebuild itself as an exact copy of pretty much what it was before the war, or maybe worse now we had the A-bomb, what happens to Sam Russo, Private Dick? He takes three rather personal hits from a gun in the hand of one of his oldest friends.

I'd had a lot of time to think things over. Truth was, all I'd done was survive my first real murder case as Sam Russo, Private Eye. I got paid to go through a kind of hellish paradise.

The paradise part was being in Saratoga Springs for the racing season. Getting to know the interesting Mrs. Willingford in a number of interesting ways wasn't too bad either.

Hell was all the rest of it.

I'd come away from Saratoga with two new and important ideas. The first was a life lesson: I liked my enemies better than my friends. It boiled down to this. Enemies were easy. You knew where you stood with 'em. In a nutshell, enemies meant you no good.

But friends? Friends were people you trusted, right? Friends were people you could count on. So was a friend some guy I shared the horrors of the Staten Island Home for Children with? Or dodged Jap artillery with? Or hung around race tracks and drank with? Who knew? I didn't, not any more. A friend tries to kill you—and almost succeeds—a person can lose sight of what friendship means. A person can wind up saying to hell with friends.

Which brought me to the second idea I'd lugged back from Saratoga's racetrack. There remained one person left in the world I knew for sure was a "friend" and that person was a dog named Jane.

Jane came with the case I'd survived. The first guy she'd loved, an up-and-coming jockey named Babe Duffy, had got himself murdered up in Saratoga Springs—and when he did, no one wanted his dog. All those no ones included me.

Duffy's dog wasn't one of those cute little mutts women like
to lug around and coo to. And she wasn't one of those big
useful brutes a lug thinks he looks manly with. Duffy's dog
was a Basenji, some sort of African dog. She was also an
acute pain in the butt.

Except for three things, name what people didn't like
about dogs and that was Jane, the African queen.

The three things were she didn't bark, she didn't slobber,
and even when soaking wet, she didn't smell like a dog.

She was mine now, or I was hers. Whichever, I think she
was happy with the arrangement. It took a little doing, but
I knew I was.

Two long months had dragged themselves by since the
end of the Saratoga Spring's horse racing season and with it
the job I'd been hired to do—solve the killings of not one,
but three young jockeys. Those two long months were spent
in Staten Island's impressive downtown Stapleton, still in the
same one room where Victory Boulevard bumped into Bay
Street lying around on the same Murphy bed.

I'd solved the case but only four people knew it. One was
me. One was the killer himself, now also as dead as his three
victims, and by the same hand: his own. One was Thomas
Clay Jefferson, the walleyed colored guy who shined shoes
in a rich white man's hotel called the Grand Union. And the
last was Mrs. Willingford.

I guess you could say Jane knew it too. It was Jane who
fingered the jockey killer because Jane was there for the
murder of one of the three jocks, namely Babe Duffy. So I
got shot by one killer and Jane got knifed by another.

Two killers. One case. This all made sense if you'd been
there.

Mrs. Willingford phoned from time to time, but as she
wasn't the type to set hoof on the isolated Isle of Staten I
didn't expect to see her soon. For one thing, there was no
racetrack or horse breeding farms. There should of been.
We had the room. I'd of really liked to see Mrs. Willingford.
Better, I'd of liked to touch Mrs. Willingford, gaze into those
hard blue eyes. But the moment she got a load of what I

called "home," all I'd get out of it was the last of a trailing silk scarf, the brim of a hat big enough for the guy carrying the world on his back at Rockefeller Center, a whiff of *L'air du Temps*, and that would be that.

I did see her doctor. She'd made the poor sap live in a local hotel so he could visit me daily, then weekly—now we were down to once a month and he was happily back where he belonged: in some snug three story brownstone in Brooklyn Heights tending to a rich kid's sniffles.

Jane saw Mrs. W's personal vet. The vet lasted longer than my doctor. Probably because the vet liked Jane and my guy could do just fine without me.

Once Thomas Clay Jefferson called to see how I was doing. I said I was doing fine. Clay said he was doing fine. Still had the same job, though things were a mite slower without the races in town. He said that was fine by him. I said I was glad it was fine by him. He said he expected me for the 1949 running of the Travers Stakes. I said I'd be there.

Twice I'd gone to the movies over at the Paramount on Bay and both times my snub nosed Colt .38 Detective Special saw the picture with me. Another effect of getting shot. I might stop carrying and I might not. Anyway, the first time was to see *Night Has a Thousand Eyes*. I'd read the book, which was terrific, so even having to leave Jane alone—Jane was a one man dog; she didn't approve of me doing something without her—the movie was a must-see considering Edward G. Robinson was in it. I wasn't all that impressed. More often than not, the book was better. This was one of those oftens. The second time I sat through *The Snake Pit*, sweating out every minute of it. Three mornings in a row now, I'd woken up thinking about the damn thing. But who could resist a title like that? Trouble was, it stirred up a lot of feelings I didn't know I had—like the fear of going nuts.

And that was my life these days. No visitors. No hanging around in bars or coffee shops. No going to the track down in Monmouth or the tracks over in Queens. No nothing.

But all this was fine by me. Except for Jane, I'd sworn off friends.

Oh crap. Now who was knocking at my door?